7 Pts

THEY
NEVER
CAME
BACK

OTHER BOOKS BY CAROLINE B. COONEY

THEY
NEVER
CAME
BACK

CAROLINE B. COONEY

DELACORTE PRESS

Copyright © 2010 by Caroline B. Cooney

All rights reserved. Published in the United States by Delacorte Press,
an imprint of Random House Children's Books, a division of
Random House, Inc., New York.

Delacorte Press is a registered trademark and the colophon is
a trademark of Random House, Inc.

Visit us on the Web! www.randomhouse.com/teens
Educators and librarians, for a variety of teaching tools,
visit us at www.randomhouse.com/teachers

Library of Congress Cataloging-in-Publication Data
Cooney, Caroline B.
They never came back / Caroline B. Cooney. — 1st ed.
p.   cm.
Summary: When fifteen-year-old Cathy decides to carpool from Norwalk to
tony Greenwich, Connecticut, to study Latin in summer school, she does not
expect the shocking events that occurred five years earlier to suddenly come
flooding back into her relatively settled life.
ISBN 978-0-385-73808-8 (trade hc) — ISBN 978-0-385-90709-5 (glb)
ISBN 978-0-375-89596-8 (e-book)
[1. Identity—Fiction. 2. Abandoned children—Fiction. 3. Foster home
care—Fiction. 4. Fugitives from justice—Fiction. 5. Embezzlement—Fiction.
6. Connecticut—Fiction.]   I. Title.
PZ7.C7834Th 2010   [Fic]—dc22   2009001368

The text of this book is set in 11.5-point Bitstream Dutch 801.
Book design by Vikki Sheatsley
Printed in the United States of America
10 9 8 7 6 5 4 3 2 1
First Edition

For my father,
Dexter Mitchell Bruce

· 1 ·

Cathy

It was the second week of summer school. The seven kids in Cathy Ferris's class were crowded around a table in the student center. Cathy opened her brown paper lunch bag to take out the sandwich she had made that morning. In the seat next to her, Ava began to frown. "Some boy from another class is staring at you, Cathy."

The attention of boys was always nice. Cathy finished the tiny act of sliding a peanut butter and banana sandwich out of its plastic bag.

Meg, sitting on the other side of Cathy, said, "Scary staring."

Cathy became aware that Graydon was upset, that Julianna was holding her breath, that Colton had set his soda can down without drinking from it, while Ethan's fork dangled in the air.

Cathy looked where they were looking.

The student center at Greenwich High was immense, with soaring ceilings, massive pillars and potted trees two stories high. Most tables, not needed for a summer school enrollment of sixty, were shoved close together at one side of the room. Fifty feet away from Cathy, a boy had risen to his feet. His eyes were glued to Cathy. He looked shocked, as if witnessing something terrible—as if Cathy were a car accident happening before his eyes.

He was tall and broad-shouldered and sturdy. His short hair was reddish blond. He looked like a jock having a meltdown. Slowly he pushed his chair out of his way and slowly moved across the open stone floor toward Cathy.

No one had ever stared at her like that. In the damp warmth of the poorly air-conditioned room, a chilly fear touched Cathy.

Even from this distance she could see that he was breathing hard, that he had lost color. Cathy found herself mirroring him. She too was shaking. Her class drew close, as if to protect her, and the cafeteria fell silent—sixty kids caught up in the boy's behavior. There was no sound except the faint squeak of his sneakers.

Cathy's fingers convulsed and crushed her brown paper lunch bag.

His eyes drilled into hers. She could not blink or move or think.

And then the boy was laughing. He turned into a happy little kid, clapping with delight. He bounced the rest of the way across the wide room. "Murielle!" he cried. "Murielle, is it *you*? It *is* you! Oh, *wow!*"

Cathy's mind was stuck. She couldn't take it anywhere.

"Murielle, it's *me*. *Tommy*. Where have you *been*?" His

arms were out. He was expecting a hug, as if they were both small children on a playground.

She couldn't remember when anybody had been this glad to see her. What should she do? What should she say? It was hard even to move her lips. "I'm Cathy," she said, but he didn't hear. He actually knelt by her chair, as if expecting to fit her with a glass slipper. "You're Murielle," he said joyfully.

Joy—at seeing *her*. Cathy's heart skittered. Then she corrected herself. Joy at seeing Murielle.

Kids were now standing up for a better view. Graydon— the oldest in Cathy's class; he would be a senior in the fall—got up from their table, squatted beside the boy and said gently, "She isn't Murielle, Tommy. Her name is Cathy Ferris. She's in my Latin class."

Graydon was a serious student. No matter how much Cathy studied, he had studied more. He had learned a truly remarkable amount of Latin in ten days. Cathy was in awe of his intelligence. If Graydon said something, it was correct. But the boy Tommy brushed Graydon away, like hair in his eyes. "I know you're Murielle," he told her. His voice broke with emotion. "Have you been in Greenwich all along?"

Now kids crossed the room to gather around Cathy's table, so they wouldn't miss anything. Cathy felt as if she should have rehearsed. But what were her lines? "I don't live in Greenwich," she told him. She could not match his dancing eyes; his happy smile. "I live in Norwalk. My town is paying tuition so I can take the accelerated language course here this summer."

3

He shook his head, beaming at her. "You're Murielle."

Cathy's fingers pleated the lunch bag, spindling the brown paper. She asked the only reasonable question. "And who is Murielle?"

Tommy sank back on his heels. His smile faded.

Graydon stood up, extended a hand and pulled Tommy to his feet. Keeping a hand on Tommy's shoulder, as if to remind Tommy that he was among friends, Graydon said to the crowd, "Murielle was his cousin. She disappeared years ago."

There was a collective gasp of horror. "Disappeared" was a hideous word. Sixty kids stared at Tommy, whose cousin had disappeared, and then all sixty pairs of eyes turned on Cathy, who looked so much like that cousin.

Tommy sagged, looking as beaten as a kid who thought he had won the big basketball game, only to lose in the last two seconds. "It was five years ago," said Tommy, still staring, his delight replaced by a dazed disappointment. "She was ten. I thought you were—" he broke off. He sighed. Then he rallied. "I'm sorry," he said to Cathy, his voice almost normal. "I don't usually attack people in public places. I was just so sure that you were Murielle."

He was still sure; she could read it in his face. "It's okay," she said lamely.

The spectators didn't give up so easily. "What happened to your cousin, Tommy?" demanded Ava. "Was she kidnapped here in Greenwich? I don't remember a kidnapping. But five years ago I was only nine. Maybe I missed it."

Ava's loud voice woke Tommy from his hypnotized stare. He seemed unnerved to find himself in a sea of

4

witnesses. Most of these kids were from Greenwich, but a dozen from area towns, like Cathy, were paying tuition to attend the summer school. They were all attempting to master an entire year of a foreign language in six weeks. Monday through Friday, they had three hours of class before lunch, three hours after lunch, and at least three hours of homework. Weekends were homework around the clock. The kids in this program wanted to display exceptional academic ability, which might catapult them into a top college. Cathy was slightly surprised to find herself in this group.

She had found the Latin class online. There were subjects she researched regularly and up had popped this unusual summer school. The guidance office at Norwalk High did all the work of getting her accepted and finding the funds. The remaining problem had been transportation, since her parents worked and could not drive her back and forth. A car pool was arranged with another commuting student. Spencer Tartaglia lived in Wilton, even farther from Greenwich than Norwalk, and his mother agreed to pick Cathy up at the Merritt Parkway exit.

Spencer had a mop of messy curls that made him easy to spot in a well-trimmed group. He was standing at the back of the lunch crowd, as fascinated as everybody. This would make much more interesting car conversation than his Arabic or Cathy's Latin.

Tommy was clearly not happy talking about his cousin's disappearance. But he had little choice. Questions were coming like pellets from a shotgun. He took a deep breath and launched himself. "Murielle was not kidnapped. My aunt and uncle, Murielle's parents, ripped off clients at their brokerage firm. Investors and pension funds lost huge amounts of money, and my aunt and uncle got away with at least ten million dollars, and maybe ten times that. Not their own money, either." His face reddened with shame. Cathy thought of all the banking and brokerage moguls to appear in the news over the last few years; people who had presented a trustworthy face but had privately jeered at their clients, and stolen every dollar in sight.

"It was a big deal at the time," said Tommy. "Lots of media coverage. My aunt and uncle fled the country so they wouldn't face trial, but their daughter, my little cousin Murielle, got left behind."

Left behind.

Every child's worst nightmare. Alone in the house without Mommy and Daddy. Running from one empty room to another.

Cathy remembered being ten years old. It was a fragile age. Ten-year-olds had to have grown-ups.

"My parents wanted her to live with us," said the boy, "but Murielle got put in foster care and vanished into the system. We went to court to get her back."

They had gone to court? Had lawyers? Faced a judge?

"But we failed," he said, as if he were still puzzled by that; still could not believe the court's decision.

"Failed" was as frightening as "left behind" or "disappeared." The sixty kids in this room had never failed. It was an alien concept.

"Murielle's probably okay," said Tommy. His voice dwindled. He was talking more to himself than to the crowd. "Or at least okay-ish, but she's lost to us."

His pain swamped Cathy. It was easier to look at her

classmates. Ava, Meg, Graydon, Ethan and Colton were transfixed by Tommy. But Julianna was watching Cathy. An expression of pure loathing crossed her face.

Cathy was jolted. It can't be me she despises. It has to be Murielle. But who could despise a ten-year-old? Especially a ten-year-old nobody's seen in five years?

"I remember that, Tommy!" cried somebody. "Your aunt and uncle—weren't they hedge fund manipulators or something? Lyman was their name. Rory and Cade Lyman. Didn't they catch a plane about five minutes before they were going to be arrested, and now they're safe in France or Namibia or Singapore?"

Tommy shrugged. "Nobody knows where they are. If federal prosecutors could figure out my aunt and uncle's location, they'd be extradited. Well, from France, anyway. I don't know about those other two countries, whether they have a treaty with the U.S. or not."

There was a rustle as people whipped out BlackBerrys and cell phones to Google the name Lyman.

"Tommy," said Ava, in her platoon sergeant voice, "do you have a photograph of Murielle? Let's compare it to Cathy and see if *we* see this resemblance."

Cathy had to end this. "I'm taking Latin," she said to Tommy, as if they were getting acquainted under normal circumstances. "What language are you taking?"

He couldn't change the subject along with her. He was blank. Somebody answered for him. "He's taking Chinese."

"When I signed up for summer school, Chinese sounded too hard. I wanted a language that uses an alphabet." She was babbling. "Preferably the alphabet I already know."

7

"Cathy!" said Ava. "You are somebody's double—and you want to talk about a dead language?"

Everybody laughed. Even Tommy laughed.

Cathy actually felt double, as if she were a paper doll waiting to be unfolded.

"There's no such thing as a double," somebody said. "Except identical twins. Anybody else is just similar."

Julianna slid to the back of the crowd where Cathy could no longer see her. Cathy felt like crying. The four girls in Latin had become friends in an hour, one of the unexpected delights of the summer. She loved being with Meg and Ava and Julianna. Surely she wasn't losing Julianna's friendship because of this!

"How do you spell 'Murielle'?" Ava asked Tommy. "I never heard it before."

Cathy was pretty sure that Ava did not care how "Murielle" was spelled; she wanted to keep on talking to Tommy. And who wouldn't? He was adorable, the perfect combination of big hunk and little kid.

"Usually it's pronounced *Mu*riel," said Tommy. "But my aunt Rory and my uncle Cade said Muri*elle*."

A little murmur ran through the group, everybody trying out the name Muri*elle*.

"I've got information on Rory and Cade Lyman," called Meg, triumphantly waving her cell. "Listen to this," she said, looking back at the information on her tiny screen. "Those two made it to England, and after that, no trace of them was ever found, *and they never came back for their kid.*"

"Don't go there," said Tommy wearily. "It's history."

8

Too late. It was now a current event. All around her, kids were texting. Cathy felt as if she were literally a news item, flung from mouth to mouth, phone to phone.

Ava said, "What kind of parents decide that money and freedom matter more than their little girl? What did they do—sit over dinner and draw up a list? Weigh the advantages? Say to each other—'Okay then: we keep the money, we bail on the kid.'"

Cathy looked down at her crushed brown paper bag. Then she shook it out and dropped the uneaten sandwich back inside. Blindly, she looked around for a trash can.

From the top of a massive curving concrete stair—one Cinderella might descend if she were a mud wrestler—came a shout. "People! Didn't you hear the bell? Time for class. Let's go, here! We're on a tight schedule."

This was a group that never willingly missed a minute of class. Immediately they were heading for their separate rooms. The Latin students waited for each other. Meg was saying, "I'm texting my dad. He's an attorney in town and he'll remember the details."

Tommy was still watching Cathy. She smiled awkwardly.

Tommy blew out his breath in a noisy huff. "The resemblance is really strong when you smile. My aunt Rory had that smile."

Cathy shut down the smile and stood there helplessly until his Chinese class dragged him off.

The kids taking Arabic, German and Latin had almost forgotten that Chinese was also being offered, because in the beginning the Chinese class had prepared their own meals as a conversational and cultural exercise. They did not come to the student center for lunch. It turned out that school insurance did not cover kids using hot stoves and smoking oil, so now they were eating with everybody else. That was why Tommy had not laid eyes on Cathy until today.

"Wow," summarized Spencer, her ride. He took the lunch bag out of her hand and threw it away for her. "You okay?" His smile was quizzical. He too was wondering if she could be Murielle Lyman.

"Just a little shaken," she said. With Tommy gone, she could let her real smile out.

Spencer grinned back. "Text me if you need to," he said. They were easy with each other, after a week and a half of carpooling. It was nice to have an ally.

At the top of the cast concrete stairs, Meg and Ava waited. No Julianna. What was going on with Julianna?

When she had caught up to them, Ava said, "Guess what? While you were fiddling with your lunch, Tommy took pictures of you on his cell phone."

"Oh?" said Cathy.

"Only one reason to do that. He still thinks you're Murielle," said Ava. "He's going to forward those pictures and get a second opinion."

· 2 ·

Murielle

Once upon a time, there had been a plain black prepaid cell phone with a single number in its address book.

Mommy handed it to Murielle early that morning, before she left for Logan Airport in Boston. She knelt beside Murielle and carefully rebraided the slippery hair that never stayed in place. "You and Daddy and I are going on a vacation in England. But the vacation is a secret, Mure. A huge big important secret. When Aunt Lois picks you up from your piano lesson, she'll drive you to the airport. You and Daddy will fly out from New York City. Meanwhile, I fly out of Boston, and we meet up in England."

It was a rare treat to travel with both parents. And if they took Murielle along on a business trip, the au pair came too, and Murielle and the au pair would tour Brussels, Milan or Geneva by themselves. But the last au pair had returned to Norway, and the new one had not yet arrived. Murielle would have Mommy and Daddy to herself.

Her parents hardly ever took vacations. Even though

they owned a house in the Hamptons and a little ranch in Wyoming and the apartment in New York, they didn't use them much. The whole idea of a family vacation was so exciting. It was what other people did: get in the car and drive a long distance and go somewhere special. "Did you pack my suitcase?" Murielle asked eagerly.

"No suitcase." Her mother was smiling. "Part of the vacation is we're going to buy everything you need in London."

Murielle's mother adored shopping. There was nothing Mommy would not buy, but Murielle didn't usually get to go with her.

"Now I've put a few things into this new backpack, and I want you to keep it closed. Don't point out to Aunt Lois that it's a new one. And this cell phone? Do not tell anybody about it, Mure. I'm going to zip it into this inside pocket. Don't let anybody, not even Aunt Lois, know that you have a second cell phone."

Murielle was puzzled. She had her own cell phone. She held it up, questioningly.

"Hang on to that, but Mommy and Daddy want you to use the new one if you need us. If there's anything like, oh, say a delay, or a traffic problem, our new number is in the address book. Don't let anybody see the new phone. Not even Cousin Tommy or your friend Kelsey. Okay?"

She wouldn't see Tommy, so it would be easy to keep the secret from him. But Kelsey? Her best best friend in fourth grade? "Okay, but—"

"It's important to keep the secret, Mure," said Daddy, giving her a kiss. "You're our partner."

He was not teasing, which was rare, and she felt proud,

and older. It's because I'm ten, she thought. If I were nine, they wouldn't make me a partner.

"Now, don't worry about anything," said Daddy. "I'll meet you at Kennedy tonight and handle everything from there. You'll never need that phone. It's just in case."

The limousine arrived. Mommy always used a driver to get to airports so she could keep working on her laptop. She was slim, taut and energetic, dressed in black, as always, and wearing high impressive heels, taking only her briefcase and a small, wheeled carry-on. She never checked baggage on a business trip.

The housekeeper drove Murielle to school, and because it was so close to the end of the school year, the day was very busy: the last testing, the final music rehearsal, the completion of art projects. Each child had a big portfolio of work done during the year, and they were to pick the best test, art, paragraph and project to display on the desktop for Parents' Night.

Parents' Night! It was tomorrow. She had forgotten to remind Mommy and Daddy!

Murielle stared at her portfolio. She was desperate to have her parents, who missed most school events, come to Parents' Night.

She could feel the weight of her turned-off regular cell phone in the pocket of her pants. She loved these pants. They were soft thin denim, peach-colored, not blue, on which tiny sparkling horses cavorted, their manes made of silver threads that Murielle liked to pleat between her fingers. Should she call? Ask Mommy and Daddy if they could fly out later and not miss Parents' Night?

"Murielle?" said her teacher. "Are you okay?"

It seemed to Murielle that the whole class turned to look at her. Her best friend Kelsey and her oldest friend Emily turned to look, and so did Chrissie, her seatmate. It seemed to Murielle that they all knew something. They could not know about the secret vacation. So what did they know?

"I'm fine," she said, and they knew she was lying. But what was the lie?

A strange creeping anxiety lodged at the base of her stomach.

At lunch, Kelsey said, "My mom told me what's happening, Murielle. She said not to bother you about it."

How could Kelsey's mother know anything?

"But she says I can invite you to stay over," Kelsey went on. "For as long as you want. Do you want to spend the weekend at my house?"

Murielle loved Kelsey's house, whose whole downstairs would fit into the Lymans' living room. It was a rough-and-tumble house, into which Kelsey and her brother and sister were allowed to bring any dog, hockey stick, muddy sneaker or tacky souvenir. They ate fast food, which Murielle loved, because her parents ate organic or not at all.

Murielle did not know how to answer Kelsey without alluding to the vacation in England. "I'll ask my mother," she said finally.

Kelsey seemed puzzled by this answer, probably because Murielle usually asked the housekeeper, Mrs. Garcia, or the au pair.

They could not discuss it further because they had an arithmetic test, and Murielle, who loved arithmetic, forgot everything in her zeal to get a hundred.

After school, the housekeeper drove Murielle to her piano lesson. "Now, your aunt Lois will pick you up," said Mrs. Garcia. "I'm making your favorite fajitas for supper. Mmm, mmm, good."

Murielle worried about this. She would not be there to eat. Mrs. Garcia would go to all that trouble for nothing. But Murielle could not explain. She had a secret to keep. She was a partner. So she waved good-bye and sat down on the piano bench. Murielle loved practice. Whether it was tennis or swimming, piano or spelling, she loved repetition. This week she had worked on her first Bach piece, a prelude in C. She loved C: it was such a cheerful key. And in this piece, the chords rolled in a satisfying warm way.

Her piano teacher said, "Murielle, I'm impressed as always. No matter what's going on, you simply practice and achieve. You're such a brave girl."

What was brave about playing the piano?

And then Aunt Lois was at the door, smiling too widely, shoveling Murielle out to the car and talking too loudly. She accelerated too fast into traffic and had to slam on the brakes. "Sorry, Muffin. I'm jittery."

"So is everybody else today."

Her aunt shot her a look but said nothing. It was not like Aunt Lois to say nothing. It was like Aunt Lois to say everything.

They got on I-95, a tough road with heavy traffic. This late in the afternoon, more cars were leaving New York City than entering it, so the beginning of their drive was not bad. But the closer they got to the Whitestone Bridge, the busier traffic became. A mile before the toll, thousands of cars came to a dead stop.

15

At Murielle's feet, the new backpack and the old book bag tipped over. The book bag was almost empty, because textbooks had been collected, there was no homework and she had returned the last school library book. She put her piano books in it, and now it was heavy and useful.

Murielle suddenly realized that Aunt Lois was crying. Through her tears Aunt Lois punched her car phone. It didn't require a headset; she just spoke and the person she called would speak back. She called Uncle Travis. "I don't think I should be doing this." Her voice was trembling.

Her uncle's voice was loud and angry. "I said so all along."

The contradictions and surprises of the day presented themselves to Murielle like a list; like a project that should be lying on her desk for Parents' Night. She pressed her little body against the seat back, and the belt tried to strangle her. Murielle slid her hand inside her jeans pocket and retrieved her cell phone. She felt safer with the phone in her hand.

"I hate her for doing this to us! She has no right!" said Aunt Lois.

"They transferred the money into our account," said her uncle. "Your sister filched one of your deposit slips so it looks as if you made the deposit. It's there whether we want it or not."

Her aunt acted as if she had to yell all the way to Greenwich. "We aren't part of this! I refuse to be part of it!"

"We're stuck now," said her uncle.

"No, we're not." Aunt Lois jerked the wheel, nosing between trucks, driving with a ferocity she never displayed.

She even drove on the forbidden shoulder and slid out an exit. Sobbing, she swerved around unknown intersections, trying to return to the highway and go the opposite direction.

"Aunt Lois," whispered Murielle. "Daddy's waiting at Kennedy. I have to fly out with him."

"No! I can't do it. I won't do it. I don't know what will become of you, but I refuse to fall into their quagmire. They want to sink—fine. I'm not sinking with them!" Aunt Lois hung a left and roared past strange little houses joined at the side, their tiny front yards closed up by chain-link fences, their tiny front steps covered by metal awnings, and then she got back on the highway. But they were now going the wrong way, speeding back to Connecticut.

Murielle tried to protest, but her aunt screamed at the top of her lungs, "Do not talk to me! I have to get through this traffic!"

Aunt Lois never yelled at Murielle.

Murielle looked behind them. On the opposite side of the divided highway, where they had been a minute ago, was a sign for Kennedy Airport. She whispered, "You could just let me out. I can walk. Or take a taxi."

Her aunt paid no attention.

Later, over the years, Murielle thought that if traffic had just been lighter, if the pace had been faster, if they had sailed through the tolls instead of inching along, Aunt Lois would not have had time to think. Murielle would have arrived at the airport and life would have been different.

But that had not happened.

"I'll call Daddy and ask him what to do," she told Aunt Lois.

"No."

"He'll be worried, Aunt Lois." Murielle opened her cell phone. "I'll miss the plane."

"Both those things would be good."

Murielle never argued with her aunt Lois. There was never anything to argue about. Her aunt was perfect and wonderful. In fact, her aunt was more fun—and, for that matter, around more—than her mother. She loved her aunt. But now she was almost afraid of Aunt Lois. She was desperate to be with her father, who would explain the whole queer day as he bought her some fun stuffed animal, and a new book, and a video for the flight.

On Murielle's phone, pictures of the people she wanted to call rather than numbers came up. She loved that. She was always finding a newer, better photograph of Mommy or Daddy.

Her aunt snatched the phone out of Murielle's hand. "Your father is a criminal fleeing the country!" she screamed. "Your mother is too! They're thieves. No matter how they pretend they're financiers caught up in a difficult year, what they do for a living is steal! My own sister has made me part of it! I hate her! I'm not doing it. And neither are you, Murielle."

Her aunt hit the window button.

A roar of wind and traffic filled the car.

Uncle Travis's voice hung in the air, tiny beady sounds forming words Murielle could not distinguish.

Aunt Lois threw Murielle's cell phone out the window.

My phone, thought Murielle. How can I call Daddy now? What will I do?

Miles later, she glanced down. At her feet sat the new backpack. Inside the zipped pocket was the secret cell phone.

"Just in case," her father had explained.

"Just in case" had arrived.

· 3 ·

Cathy

"*Tacete!*" said the Latin teacher, but the students were too stirred up for silence.

Ava explained to Mrs. Shaw. "A boy named Tommy from the Chinese class thought Cathy was his long-lost cousin Murielle! He came running over during lunch and literally fell to his knees, begging her to be Murielle. According to him, Cathy is Murielle's double."

Ethan propped his open laptop in front of Cathy. "*Greenwich Time* Web site," he identified. "Newspaper coverage from the week Rory and Cade Lyman disappeared."

"That must have been Tommy Petrak, then," said Mrs. Shaw, moving forward to close the lid of Ethan's laptop. "The Lyman scandal was big news for a while. They had investments everywhere. Property and—" Mrs. Shaw seemed to miss a beat. She backed away. Her hands darted around until they located papers on her desk. She fiddled with them.

Ethan took his laptop back. "Maybe you're a separated identical twin, Cathy," he said. "Were you adopted?"

"This isn't a great topic," said Graydon. He looked flushed and upset. "Tommy's mom and dad were in trouble too. They were accused of helping the aunt and uncle flee prosecution and get out of the country. If they'd been found guilty, they'd have faced jail time. That's why the little girl was taken away and put into foster care. Everybody thought Tommy's parents would be indicted."

Ava slid a note into Cathy's lap. It was in Latin. Cathy was too rattled to decipher it. *Amo notiam geminae.* "I love the something of something."

Mrs. Shaw confiscated the note. "'I love the idea of a twin,'" she translated. "You get points for the Latin, Ava, but we have to accomplish more than a week's worth of class every day. We cannot linger over mistaken identities. Page one-oh-two in your Wheelock. *Audite diligenter.*"

Cathy could not listen at all, never mind diligently. Her thoughts were like skittish horses, impossible to catch. She couldn't even look around. Julianna's eyes had fixed on her, hot with dislike.

"Cathy?" said the teacher. *"Converte hanc sententiam ex Latino in Anglicum."*

Cathy was supposed to translate a sentence from Latin to English? Now?

Ava murmured a clue. Cathy's brain slid into gear. Latin was as orderly as arithmetic. She made her brain as thin and sharp as a pencil and pointed herself at the Latin. Other people multitasked. Cathy single-tasked. It had saved her many times.

Latin itself, solid and predictable and nicely arranged, came to the rescue. She leaned on the Latin.

An hour later, Mrs. Shaw gave them a ten-minute

break. Cathy had not even closed her Wheelock when Colton was standing over her with his cell phone. Colton, who never talked unless Mrs. Shaw called on him, confided, "I told my dad what happened, and since he knew Rory and Cade Lyman, I sent him your picture to see if he sees the resemblance."

Colton had taken her picture too? She had gone from least visible class member to most interesting forwarding material? Cathy could feel herself losing weight, as these people made off with pieces of her.

Colton read his father's text message out loud. "'I didn't know there was a child involved. I barely remember what the Lymans look like so can't help with any possible resemblance to Murielle.'"

"I don't care for the name Murielle," said Meg. "It's heavy and old-fashioned."

"Old names are in style," said Ava. "In my homeroom last year, there were a Maud, an Emma and a Gladys."

"Gladys?" repeated Meg, laughing. "Ugh. Is her personality warped?"

Ava poked her. "No more than mine."

Light banter was one of Cathy's specialties. But even though she seemed to lose weight and substance just sitting here, she did not feel light.

"I can't wait to get home and do research," said Ethan. "This is better than a television show. I want to know how anybody can vanish in Europe or America when you have to have photo identification and ID numbers and thumbprints, and video cameras are everywhere, and you carry your credit history around and banks track your deposits." Ethan sent himself a list of things to check.

22

I'm his research, thought Cathy. Then she pulled herself together. The Lymans were his research.

"Cathy," asked Meg, "how come we're the ones who are excited when you're the possible long-lost cousin?"

She tried to show a little excitement, but the outlines of Murielle's fate were too frightening.

"You don't want to be Murielle, do you?" said Julianna. She didn't seem angry anymore. She had probably never been angry. Cathy had dreamed up emotions reflected off Tommy's intensity.

"It was a little . . ." Cathy searched for a word, decided against "creepy" and said, "disturbing."

Julianna's eyes were out of focus, as if she were elsewhere. "Tommy's nice," she said. "We've been in class together since kindergarten. He didn't mean to upset you."

"Tommy's adorable," said Ava. "He couldn't take his eyes off you, Cathy. I bet he's sitting in Chinese staring at your picture. I bet he waits for you after school, Cathy."

"You have to take advantage of that," said Meg.

Mrs. Shaw stopped the conversation. "We're going to do our first real translation, people. A paragraph of Cicero."

Cathy could not possibly fall backward two thousand years, not when she was trapped in Tommy's dashed hopes. On his knees, he had begged her to be Murielle! What if she had said, "Yes, I'm your cousin Murielle." What would have happened?

Ava read aloud. *"Quid facis, Catilina? Quid cogitas? Sentimus magna vitia insidiasque tuas."*

"It really is a dead language when you read like that, Ava. Come on, put a little zip into it. It's sixty-three BC. A criminal is sauntering into the Senate, knowing that nobody dares to punish him, because he is too dangerous and too powerful. And you, Cicero, are towering with rage, not just at Catiline, the criminal, but at the whole Senate, because they are all weaklings."

Ava read again, with zest.

"Julianna?" said Mrs. Shaw. "Translation?"

Julianna was totally into it. She spat out the words. "What are you doing, Catiline? What are you thinking? We know your great crimes and your treachery."

They were all inside the Latin now. Mrs. Shaw and Ava and Julianna had them sitting on their stone seats in their white togas, as Cicero accused Catiline of conspiracy.

At 3:14, Mrs. Shaw said, "You can be proud. Tuesday of our second week, after only seven class days, and you are reading Cicero. Condensed and simplified, to be sure, but you did it."

Condensed and simplified? They hadn't done the real thing? Everybody was disappointed. But then it was 3:15, the day was over and books were slammed shut. Every kid but Cathy turned on a cell phone to check and send messages. Cathy had a cell, but her minutes were limited, and she wanted to wait until she was home to call her friends. She might not call them at all. They were puzzled by her decision to commute to Greenwich just to study a dead language. But mostly they were annoyed. She and her best friends were on the tennis team. They were not amused when Cathy claimed to have no time to play this summer. Was she picking rich Greenwich kids over her true Norwalk friends?

The seven Latin students moved down the huge solid

stairs into the student center. High on the walls hung long rows of international flags, as if this were the United Nations. Perhaps during the regular school year it was; Greenwich was *the* town where foreign diplomats and executives had homes, leaving their families every day for the commute to Manhattan.

The name Murielle Lyman floated up from the loudly chattering kids below her. Everyone who had seen Tommy Petrak cross the cafeteria had texted or called parents, friends, brothers, sisters and other contacts, demanding information about Rory and Cade Lyman, and asking for a picture of their little girl, to see if Cathy Ferris really was Murielle's double. Nobody had turned up a file photo of Murielle, so five years ago, the media had been kind. They hadn't blamed the little girl for her parents.

Cathy descended the stairs. Everybody took another look at the possible child of celebrity fugitives.

She searched the crowd for Spencer. Mrs. Tartaglia had made it clear that while she was willing to drive Cathy, she was not thrilled. A car pool restricted her. What if she wanted to be late or early, or had errands to run? Spencer had promised to keep his mom in line, but Cathy didn't want to test her.

Through the student center and down the long front hall they trooped. Kids poured out rows of glass doors into a courtyard large enough to be a city square. Sun baked the bricks. Tall exotic grasses, their plumes and spots like camouflage for wild animals, waved in the hot wind. Beyond stone benches was a row of waiting cars. There were too few kids in summer school for buses to run. Older students drove their own cars, and parents came for the rest.

Cathy realized that yet more kids were taking pictures of her on their cell phones. Weird. Then suddenly it was funny, and Cathy was laughing. Who could have anticipated this?

"Told you," said Ava, pointing. "Tommy's waiting for you."

Tommy was standing in the sun, flanked by a tall thin man and a short heavy woman who were peering into the school with that excited, shade-your-eyes squint people use in airports when they're searching for a loved one coming out the gate.

"Tommy's parents," said Julianna, in case there was any doubt. "The Petraks. They're not here to pick Tommy up. He has his own car. They're here for you, Cathy. They think you're Murielle too."

· 4 ·

Murielle

H er parents? Thieves?

Murielle dismissed this crazy talk from her aunt Lois. Her mother and father would never steal anything. As for "fleeing the country"—what did that even mean?

Aunt Lois was Mommy's older sister. They bickered a lot, but mostly they had fun. Mommy did not have time for friends. She and Daddy worked in their office at home, or in the office in Greenwich, or in the other office near Wall Street. They always meant to socialize. They had been talking about buying a new house on a golf course. They didn't actually like golf; it took too much time. They liked tennis, which was fast. They saved themselves the trouble of finding partners by playing against each other, on their own court.

Aunt Lois was the one who could put together a picnic at Island Beach or a trip to the Bruce Museum. Aunt Lois knew when the nature center in Stamford had a special event or the skating pond in Binney Park had frozen over.

Whenever both Daddy and Mommy had business trips, Murielle liked to stay with Aunt Lois rather than the housekeeper and the au pair. She always hoped to play with her cousin Tommy, who was two years older. More and more these days, Tommy wouldn't bother with her. A twelve-year-old boy had better things to do than entertain a ten-year-old girl cousin.

Aunt Lois was too upset to drive well. Twice she ran out of her lane and over the rumble strip. The car phone began to ring.

It's Daddy, thought Murielle. He'll tell Aunt Lois to turn around, and I'll still make the plane.

Three rings went by. Four.

Murielle's stomach knotted. Stomach knots were a constant problem. When she was nervous, she couldn't even lift food to her mouth, never mind chew. Sometimes she couldn't even be in the room with food.

Aunt Lois punched the phone on. "Cade?" she demanded, as if hoping the word would cut his throat.

"Hey, Lo," said Daddy cheerfully. He always called Aunt Lois Lo. He sounded as if he were right in the car with them. Murielle relaxed. "You guys running late, Lo?"

"I turned around. I'm not doing this. You and Rory do what you want, but you're not dragging me into it and you're not dragging Muffin into it. She'll live with us."

Muffin was Aunt Lois's nickname for her. Her parents called her Mure.

Now her father shouted too. Aunt Lois shouted back. It was like being in the midst of gunfire. What could Aunt

Lois possibly mean by "she'll live with us"? Murielle whispered, "Let me talk to him, Aunt Lois."

"No!" Her aunt hung up.

Murielle sat very still. Now Daddy would call Murielle on the very cell phone Aunt Lois had hurled out the window. That phone was now crushed plastic. The special backup phone was not turned on. In front of Aunt Lois, Murielle could not take it out of the backpack. Not just because of the secret, but because Aunt Lois might throw away the second phone too.

They were almost back in Greenwich. Murielle decided to carry her book bag and backpack upstairs to the bedroom she always had and call Daddy on the special cell phone. If he got hold of their usual car service, the driver could get her to the airport in time for the flight. If it took too long, Daddy could just rearrange their departure time for a later flight.

When Aunt Lois pulled into her driveway, Uncle Travis and Cousin Tommy were standing there.

Tommy, desperate to find a sport in which he would be a star, was trying baseball, soccer, tennis, golf, lacrosse and water polo. He was too busy to stand around and wait for his mother's car to arrive.

Aunt Lois stopped the car. She forgot to put it in park, so the car lurched dangerously and she swore, which Murielle had never heard her do. "Murielle," said her aunt, in a low ugly voice, "tomorrow or the day after, people will ask questions about your mother and father. And they will ask questions about me. You must not tell anybody we were headed to the airport. Do you understand me? I ran errands after I picked you up at your piano lesson. Do not mention the airport. We don't know anything about an airport." She was screaming by the time Uncle Travis opened Murielle's door.

"Hi, Muffin," he said tiredly. He led her inside. Aunt Lois and Tommy scuffed along after them.

In the front hall, her uncle took away her book bag and backpack and hung them on hooks in the big coat closet. My phone, thought Murielle. But she didn't argue. She didn't want Uncle Travis to think that the backpack was extra important.

He gave the closet door a halfhearted push. It did not fully close, but it did hide the contents. "Tommy, take Muffin down to the playroom and keep her busy. Your mother and I have to talk."

Her legs felt like sticks. Her knees didn't bend. She didn't think she could make it down the stairs. She had to call Daddy. Ask him what was happening.

Uncle Travis and Aunt Lois went into the kitchen.

"Did they tell you anything?" asked Tommy.

She shook her head.

"They didn't tell me anything either. But at school everybody's talking about it. It was in the papers and on TV. Did the other kids give you a hard time, Muffin? You don't have to go back to school tomorrow if you don't want. The year's almost over anyway."

She stared at him, but his own phone had begun to ring, and he pulled it out and looked at it. "It's Uncle Cade!" he exclaimed, as if this were extraordinary. As if nobody on earth ever got a call from Murielle's father.

Murielle had not even had time to be happy that Daddy

was calling when Aunt Lois raced out of the kitchen, snatched the phone out of Tommy's hand and screamed, "How dare you telephone my son! How dare you drag him into this!"

Murielle's brain stiffened. It wasn't soft and thinky. It was a slab, hard and scared.

Finally her aunt's voice softened. "Cade, make this easy for Muffin. Do the right thing." She handed Murielle the phone.

The anxiety that usually attacked Murielle's stomach now entered her throat. After a few swallows, the only word she could say was "Daddy?"

"Hey, Mure. This isn't how it was supposed to go. But it did. So here's the deal. Mommy already caught her plane out of Boston and Daddy has to be on this flight out of Kennedy. You stay with Aunt Lois for a day or two and we'll figure out how to get you. Be my brave girl, and don't worry about what people say, okay?"

"Okay."

"I love you, honey," said her father.

"Okay."

"I have to board, Mure."

"Okay."

"I'll see you soon," said her father.

"Okay."

Murielle was left with a dial tone.

Why hadn't she said, "I love you, too"? Why hadn't she said, "No, Daddy, call the car service, I can still make the plane"? Why hadn't she said, "Tell me what's happening! I can help"?

That night she ate nothing, but no one noticed. Aunt

31

Lois, who loved to cook, never fixed dinner. Tommy nuked something for himself and Uncle Travis grazed on leftovers while Aunt Lois scarfed down a party-size bag of chips and then started on ice cream straight from the carton.

Her aunt and uncle never turned the lights off that night. Never went to bed. They just argued. They came upstairs constantly to check on Murielle, as if they thought she was up to something. She wasn't. She had been on a lot of plane flights. Phones were turned off once the plane was in the air. A flight to England would last six or eight hours. There was no point sneaking downstairs and trying to get the phone out of the new backpack when Mommy's and Daddy's phones were off.

Murielle was amazed to wake up in the morning, because that meant she had slept. In fact, overslept. She was late for school. She leaped out of bed, hoping she had left clothes at this house that were good enough for school.

Her aunt stood in the doorway. "Tommy already left. He was up in time for the bus."

If I'd caught the plane, she thought dizzily, I'd miss school anyway. So it doesn't matter if I go to school.

"I should take you to school," said Aunt Lois in a thin voice. "We need to look normal. Do you want to go to school?"

Murielle always wanted to go to school. She loved school. But at school, there would be no chance to use the special cell phone. Better to stay here, wait until Aunt Lois was not looking, call Daddy and find out when they were coming for her.

Aunt Lois picked up a brush and set to work on Murielle's hair. Murielle didn't have much hair, and it never looked like much either. It just slid out of its braids and hung around.

Downstairs, the doorbell rang.

Aunt Lois edged over to a window. "It's them."

"Who?"

"I'm going to tell them they can't question you," said Aunt Lois. "You're just a little girl. But if they question you anyway, remember: we were not going to the airport."

· 5 ·

Cathy

The parents of Thomas Petrak moved toward Cathy, half sobbing, half laughing. They were hoping Cathy would say, "Yes! You've found me! I'm Murielle!"

Sixty teenagers pretended to head for their cars, but in fact, paused to watch and listen. Their slow-motion walk was eerie, as if choreographed.

Mrs. Tartaglia tapped her horn. Spencer dashed over. He was as nervous as the Petraks. "Sorry," he whispered loudly, as if in a funeral home. "Mom has a hair appointment," he said, both to the Petraks and Cathy. "We have to leave now so we can get there in time."

Mrs. Petrak ignored him. She stretched out her hands. "Murielle! Oh, Muffin, sweetheart! I'm so glad you're all right. It's me. Aunt Lois."

Cathy was flooded by the emotion pouring out of Mrs. Petrak, whose joy and relief were like banners, snapping in Cathy's face.

Mrs. Tartaglia honked again.

Spencer said nervously, "I'm really sorry, Mrs. Petrak. But this is actually Cathy Ferris, and we're her ride and we have to leave." He tried to joke. "My mom misses her hair appointment and the world collapses."

Mrs. Petrak waved Spencer away. "We'll give Murielle a ride home. Don't worry. You go on." Mrs. Petrak's hair did not appear to receive attention at a beauty parlor. She was plump and imperfectly dressed and the colors of her clothing clashed. But she was beautiful. Her outstretched arms attracted Cathy the way a magnet attracts iron filings. Cathy yearned to give Mrs. Petrak the hug she wanted so badly. But she didn't.

Tommy was beside himself. "I was wrong," he said to his parents. "She isn't Murielle. Her name is Cathy Ferris. I shouldn't have sent her picture to you. I'm sorry," he said to Cathy. "Mom," he said to his mother, "back off, okay?"

Tommy's mother needed to touch Cathy. Her fingers were almost on Cathy's skin. Cathy stepped back. Mrs. Petrak's joy became pain. Cathy felt small and mean.

Spencer said, "Uh, Cathy? I'll tell Mom you'll be a few minutes, okay?"

Tommy's father held out his hand in the normal way, for her to shake. "I'm Travis Petrak, Cathy. You have a startling resemblance to our missing niece."

She let him pump her hand. She found her voice. She even managed a protest. "You haven't seen your niece in five years, Tommy said. And she was just a little girl."

Thomas's mother removed a five-by-seven silver frame from her large handbag and held it out. Cathy took it.

A man and a woman were sitting on a porch swing, green leaves behind them, red flowers beside them. The woman looked as if every calorie she ate vanished instantly into excitement and energy. A wide grin lifted thin cheeks. Short curly hair almost bounced. The man was handsome in the way of somebody modeling sports clothing. His blond hair was thick, his muscles ready and his skin glowing. His grin sat sideways, as if he should have had some important orthodontic procedure in his teens. It gave him an impish look. The man and woman were an enticing couple. You knew you'd have a blast with these two.

Between them sat a small dark child who didn't look like much of anything. She was just a kid. The parents seemed more aware of the camera than of the child. And yet the three made a beautiful composition. The picture leaped with affection and pleasure.

Mrs. Tartaglia arrived on the scene. "A fascinating situation," she said loudly, "and of course you'll want to follow up on it, but not now. I have to leave and Cathy has to leave with me." She moved between Cathy and Mrs. Petrak like a sheepdog separating the flock.

"No, no," said Mrs. Petrak. "Wait."

Mrs. Tartaglia was not interested. "Cathy, give these people your phone number so you can handle this later." To Tommy's mother she said, "There's definitely been a mix-up. I've met the parents."

Cathy had to scurry to keep up with Mrs. Tartaglia. She felt too disorganized even to open the back door of the Lexus, never mind recite a phone number. She glanced over her shoulder. Mrs. Petrak was weeping. She waved, as if Cathy were a little girl going off to kindergarten. As for

Tommy, he was so embarrassed Cathy figured he'd drop out of summer school.

She sank into the backseat. How cold, how cruel she had been. She should have handled this better.

"What happened?" demanded Mrs. Tartaglia, accelerating. There were two routes home: the parkway, which was north of Greenwich High, and the interstate, which was south. Mrs. Tartaglia took an iffy right turn on red and sped toward the simply named North Street. It wasn't a simple street. It was lined with mansions and estates, landscaped vistas and long driveways leading to palatial houses deep within the trees. This was one of the wealthiest towns in America, and it showed.

"You know what happened, Mom. I told you," said Spencer.

"I want detail, Spence. Cathy, you tell me. You're the double."

"I haven't thought it through yet," she said. This was an understatement. She didn't even know how to begin thinking this through. "How about Spencer tells and I listen too?"

So Spencer told. "Plus," he finished up, "there's this girl in Cathy's class named Julie."

"Julianna," Cathy corrected him. Her skin prickled. Had Spencer found out why Julianna loathed a missing ten-year-old?

"Well," said Spencer, getting to the good part, "our language teacher remembered everything about the Lymans. Julianna's mother, Nancy Benner, was the manager of Rory and Cade Lyman's Greenwich office. It turns out that Greenwich was hedge fund central five years ago. There was as much going on there as on Wall Street. Anyway, Julianna's mother knew what the Lymans were up to, and when they skipped town, she was the one left holding the bag. Or, actually, the accounting procedures. She went to prison. Just for two years, and she's out now, but the Benners lost everything, including their house, and the girls in my class said that the Benners are living in a tiny apartment over somebody's garage, and they only have that because somebody in their church is being nice to them."

Cathy almost threw up.

Even two hours in a prison must feel like forever. But two *years*? What could be more horrifying than your own mother in a cage, surrounded by the cages of others? *For two years*.

"Julianna didn't tell us that," said Cathy. She fought off a sob.

"Well, no," said Mrs. Tartaglia. "Like you'd announce that in class."

I bet Mrs. Shaw remembered that too, thought Cathy. That's why she cut off her explanation of property and investment. And Graydon was just pretending it was hard on Tommy, because he knew it was much harder on Julianna. I bet the other kids in Latin don't know about Nancy Benner, though. We have a big age spread and even the Greenwich kids went to different middle schools, or maybe weren't living there five years ago, and the high school has more than two thousand kids. You wouldn't cross paths with half of them, let alone know their histories.

"People aren't going to let go of this possible-double thing, Cathy," said Spencer. "It's too cool. They'll look up everything there is on Rory and Cade Lyman, and they'll find the trial of Nancy Benner. Julianna will have to deal with it tomorrow in school."

You would think scars like that would show. But Julianna looked like anybody else. Except prettier. Now Julianna would have to endure public humiliation all over again, just because Cathy Ferris decided to go to summer school.

Mrs. Tartaglia studied Cathy in the rearview mirror. "So? Are you Murielle?"

"Mom!" said Spencer. "You talked to Mr. and Mrs. Ferris when the car pool was set up."

"They could have adopted her."

"If a person is adopted at ten," said Spencer, "the person knows. Plus the actual parents, Rory and Cade Lyman, must still be alive. You can't adopt anybody if their parents are still alive, can you?"

Still alive, thought Cathy. Out there somewhere, on the run, without their little girl.

"They never came back?" asked Mrs. Tartaglia, marveling that anybody could be so cruel to their little girl.

"They never came back," agreed Spencer.

Ava's right, thought Cathy. They must have made an actual decision one day, after an actual discussion. Keep the money; bail on the kid.

"I'm glad, Cathy," said Mrs. Tartaglia, roaring up one of the beautiful hills of the parkway, "that you are not related to these Lyman people. They're probably on some

Mediterranean isle, living high and having fun while others pay the price. Greed is their middle name. It's just as well that you did not give those Petrak people your phone number. I foresee difficulties ahead. Do you want me to alert your parents?"

· 6 ·

Murielle

Murielle followed Aunt Lois down the stairs. The visitors peered through the slender windows on either side of the front door, like kids at Halloween. It didn't seem like a grown-up thing to do.

"Stay upstairs," Aunt Lois ordered her.

But the special cell phone was down here. Murielle, who was always a good girl, did not obey.

Aunt Lois would take the visitors into the living room, which was relatively neat and clean, as opposed to the rest of the house, which was untidy and needed vacuuming. Aunt Lois had no household help. At Murielle's, people from the maid service were always showing up—polishing, scouring, dusting, mopping. Murielle had not gotten to know any of them, and they never seemed interested in getting to know her either: they just wanted to scrub the showers and leave. Murielle's house sparkled.

But Aunt Lois's house was easy to live in.

The minute these visitors and Aunt Lois were in the living room, Murielle would get her backpack out of the hall closet, tiptoe upstairs and call her parents.

Aunt Lois opened the front door.

There were four visitors. They were a team, they explained, from the DOJ, the FBI, the SEC and the NASD. Murielle was familiar with the letters FBI, but she didn't know the others.

Aunt Lois did not invite the initial people in. She stood there, saying yes, Rory Lyman was her sister. No, she could not guess where Rory Lyman was. Yes, Cade Lyman was her brother-in-law. No, she did not know where Cade Lyman was.

Why did these strangers want to know where Mommy and Daddy were? It could not be a good thing that the FBI wanted to talk to them.

There was something dreadful about how Aunt Lois stood in the door, spreading herself, as if she thought the initials people would try to ooze in between her legs.

Was Aunt Lois telling the truth? She might be. Aunt Lois knew Daddy and Mommy had flown away yesterday. But maybe she didn't know the flight or the airline or the destination. Murielle knew three things. Her parents had landed by now. They were in England. Her father would come for her soon.

Behind Murielle, the door to the kitchen was cracked. Uncle Travis was hiding behind it, peeking.

Murielle felt like Alice in Wonderland drinking from the wrong bottle. Nobody was behaving the way they were supposed to.

She forgot which initials went with which visitor. She

couldn't tell them apart. Three men and a woman were weirdly identical. The same height, the same frown.

"No," Aunt Lois was saying, "this is not my daughter. This is my niece."

The initial people stared at Murielle.

One man said, "Hi, honey. I'm Matt Keefer. You can call me Matt. I need to talk to your mom and dad. Can you tell me where they are?"

"You leave her alone," said Aunt Lois. "Murielle, go to your room."

Maybe she should. Maybe the phone had to wait.

"Can we take a look at your cell phone, Muriel?" asked Matt Keefer. He pronounced her name wrong. People usually did. Murielle had to coach them to get the accent right. "See, Muriel, there might be a phone number on your cell that we could use."

The worst thing would be for Matt Keefer to find out about the new cell phone. Murielle's fear stuck to her, damp and smelly, like a wet bathing suit.

Aunt Lois said shrilly, "She doesn't have a cell phone."

The initial people were skeptical. All kids had cell phones, especially rich kids, especially rich kids whose parents were away a lot and would keep in touch with phone calls and texts and voice messages.

Matt Keefer said conversationally, "We know that Mom and Dad flew out of separate airports last night and landed safely in England."

Murielle was the only child in fourth grade who still called her parents Mommy and Daddy. "Mom and Dad" sounded like other people's parents. She did not feel very involved with "Mom and Dad."

43

"We know that Dad had a ticket for you, Muriel. He expected you to be on the same flight out of New York."

"You leave her alone," said Aunt Lois. "Whatever my sister did, my niece had nothing to do with it. Murielle, go upstairs."

Murielle just stared at them.

"You've terrified her," said Aunt Lois. "It's fine, honey. Don't worry about a thing." Her voice climbed an octave and then broke.

"May we come in and talk, Mrs. Petrak?" said the female initials person. She was getting mad. And Aunt Lois was getting scared. Her grip on the edge of the front door loosened. After a while, she backed up. They walked in.

Matt Keefer studied Murielle. Murielle studied her shoes. They were not her favorites. She had worn these yesterday because they were easy to kick off at the security gate in the airport.

Aunt Lois's voice quavered. "If you'll come with me into the living room . . ."

She led the way. Uncle Travis crept out of the kitchen and followed the visitors into the living room.

Murielle opened the closet door, which made no noise, since it had never been fully closed, took her backpack and book bag off their hooks and hurried upstairs. She hung the bags on hooks in her own closet, between a fluffy pink robe and a towel printed with unicorns. She didn't like unicorns anymore, but Aunt Lois did not follow fashion and was not constantly buying new. The unicorn towel would hang here forever, even when it frayed, and Aunt Lois would not notice. Mommy, on the other hand, would

44

be excited that Murielle no longer liked unicorns and would throw the towel in the trash, and off they would go in search of new everything.

It was hot in her little bedroom. Aunt Lois didn't have central air, and this room didn't even have a window unit. The two windows were open a few inches, but no breeze came through. There was a ceiling fan, but Murielle did not have time to flick a switch. She unzipped the inside pocket, retrieved the new cell phone and turned it on. It was black and boring and slimmer than her real phone.

It blinked with messages. They would be from Mommy and Daddy, because nobody else knew about the phone. But there was no time to listen. She had to warn them about the FBI. She pressed Contacts and up came two choices: Mommy. Daddy.

She turned to Mommy for important things. But it was Daddy she had talked to last—if you could call it talking. She hadn't even said "I love you." Daddy's feelings might be hurt. She should call Daddy.

But it was Mommy she wanted.

She moved her thumb to press Send and heard a heavy footstep down at the bottom of the stairs. It was not Aunt Lois, who was light on her feet, and played tennis as well as Rory, even though she weighed seventy-five pounds more than her sister. It was not Uncle Travis, who believed that stairs were good for your heart and always charged up.

"Muriel?" called Mr. Keefer. "Can I come up?"

Her bedroom door was open. He would climb ten steps, turn left, take two steps and be in here. Murielle could not just stuff the phone in her pocket. It would show. She moved her thumb to a different key and pressed, turning the phone off, because if it rang, they would follow the sound.

At home she had a suite including playroom, reading nook, dressing room and bathroom. But her room at Aunt Lois's was small and sparsely furnished. There was no place to hide anything.

Murielle imitated Aunt Lois.

She threw the phone out the window. She would get it later. This was not a family of gardeners; nobody was going to be out in the shrubbery pruning. Nor did they hire landscapers. The lawn got mowed when the neighbors got annoyed. The cell phone would be fine in the grass. Later on, Murielle would offer to play outside, and what grown-up argued with exercise and fresh air? Once Murielle had put some distance between herself and these people with their initials, she could call Mommy.

But Murielle was at an awkward angle and the window was open only a few inches. The phone did not fly out onto the grass. It slid down the roof and into the gutter.

It was visible.

Murielle stepped away from the window, reached for a book, flipped it open and flopped onto the bed.

"Knock, knock," said Mr. Keefer, smiling. "Can we have a little chat?"

· 7 ·

Cathy

All the students had left.
    All the cars were gone.

The school had that hot abandoned look of summer. Just brick and stones and silence.

"She's Murielle," said Lois Petrak, who had not yet moved. "She even called you Tommy."

His mother's emotions had tapered off only a little. Dad had driven away, too upset to take any more. Tommy had yet to coax his mother into his own car. He felt as if she might stand here till the sun went down, staring at the spot where Cathy had stood. "She called me Tommy because I introduced myself as Tommy," he said patiently. "Anyway, I haven't convinced anyone to start saying Thomas. They all say Tommy."

"She's Murielle. We're going to the administration office. I need the file on her."

"Mom, you can't pursue this. Cathy's just a passerby and I went a little crazy when I thought I saw a resemblance."

"You did see a resemblance. So did I. She's Murielle."

Murielle's fate was the tragedy of his mother's life; worse by far than what her sister Rory had done. His mother still prayed for this little girl they didn't have and never would. And now, thanks to his stupidity, Mom was going to bulldoze into poor Cathy Ferris's life. Cathy had been polite about it, but how would she feel if this went on and on?

He well knew how the media, neighbors, classmates, friends and strangers were riveted by the concept of somebody vanishing and creating a new but hidden life. As long as you didn't think too hard about the fact that the Lymans' escape was made with stolen money, you could see it as some great adventure. Everybody wanted to skate on the edge of it and watch it unfold.

But the Petraks were not on the edge. They were in the middle.

In the blistering sun, Tommy felt himself at risk. Nothing about Rory and Cade and their disappearance had been clear or clean. They had left broken lives behind them. His mother had not been broken, but she had been damaged. What if the nightmare resurfaced? He hated Rory and Cade for continuing to cast a shadow five years later. He hated himself for being an emotional idiot and hurling himself across the room in front of all those witnesses.

To his relief, the headmaster was not in. The secretary snarled at them. "We do not give out personal information on our students," she said to Mrs. Petrak, as if they were discussing possible arson.

But it could be arson, thought Tommy. Cathy Ferris's life could go up in smoke.

———

48

Julianna could not drag herself up the outdoor wooden stairs that led to the garage apartment. She felt stripped of soul and strength. Safe solid Latin, invaded by Rory and Cade Lyman. There was no end to the ripple effect of those crimes.

It wasn't fair to be mad at Tommy. But he had now ensured that every kid in summer school would take on the Lyman saga like an extra-credit project.

A floor above Julianna, her mother opened the apartment door and smiled down. It was not the huge happy smile that poor Mrs. Petrak had worn for so short a time. But it was the same need to touch. In prison, you cannot touch. Your arms do not encircle your child.

Julianna hoped that Rory and Cade Lyman knew every minute of every day that they could not touch their missing daughter. She hoped they suffered.

She had often wondered about the fate of Murielle. Ten years old was so little. Julianna knew what it was to realize that your own parent was the bad guy. But imagine if you also had to understand that your mother and father cared more about freedom than about you. Imagine gradually figuring out that you would live with strangers for the rest of your life.

When the long hug with her mother ended, Julianna set her book bag neatly in its slot. The garage apartment was so small for four people. Either you put stuff away or you tripped over it.

Julianna's hobby was baking. Such a soothing activity, and good stuff to show for it. Rich enticing smells and yummy results. She loved the bowls and spoons, the rolling pin and the shine of the cookie sheets.

"How was your day?" asked her mother eagerly. There was a tiny breakfast bar, with only two stools. Aiden and her mother took the stools. They loved watching Julianna bake. Aiden would put dibs on the bowl, because he loved raw dough.

Julianna flipped open the King Arthur Flour cookbook to the molasses cookie recipe. The spices gave off such a cheerful scent.

"My day," she said, "was not what I expected." She told them about Tommy and the possible double. She had to. There would be repercussions from this, although as yet Julianna could not tell what they would be. But her brother and her mother might need to brace themselves.

The Benners had been through hell, and it showed no sign of ending. Her mother's shame and fury had been sharpened, not dulled, by two years in the women's prison in Niantic. Julianna's father was staying only for the children's sake. Julianna didn't care why he stayed. She just knew she could not get through life without both parents.

She and Aiden had to coax and jockey and maneuver their parents to keep them steady. This was going to set her mother off something fierce. Julianna dreaded having to tell Dad.

"Do you think she is Murielle?" asked Aiden.

"How could she be? She's registered at school. Her name is Cathy Ferris. You wouldn't believe how into it our class is. Meg and Ava are research pit bulls. Graydon knows everything already, and he tried to chill everybody out, but of course that didn't work. Even Colton and Ethan, who are total duds, were Googling and texting and discussing how they would vanish if they had to, and

50

offering theories about the Lymans. Cathy herself just changed the subject."

"Cathy sounds mature," said her mother. "Why would she want to be related to Rory and Cade Lyman? Any more than you want to be related to me."

"Oh, Mom, cut it out. I love you."

They had all paid such a price. The year before the trial, the two years Mom was in prison and the first year after Mom was released, Julianna felt as if the whole family were behind bars. Every time she remembered the long traffic-jammed drives up 95 to the prison for their weekly visits, she wanted to run screaming into some other life. She tried not to resent Tommy for throwing her history into summer school, where everything had been safe and scholarly. Even now her classmates would be turning up the name Nancy Benner and reading about how Murielle was not the only one left behind: Rory and Cade had left Nancy Benner to face the music.

It was such a strange phrase: "face the music." There had been no music in the investigation, trial and imprisonment of Nancy Benner.

If only they had moved away. But their father believed the Greenwich schools had no equal and wanted Aiden and Julianna to stay here.

"Is Cathy nice?" asked Aiden.

"If she is," said their mother, "then she's not the daughter of Rory and Cade."

"You thought the world of them at the time."

Her mother nodded. "They were so exciting. It was so much fun. They would say, 'We're skating on the edge today!' And I'd laugh, and they'd laugh, and we'd do something iffy. Not illegal, but risky. And when we were facing huge losses and knew we could go under, we kept saying, 'We have to do this one little thing to save ourselves. Not a big deal—we'll pull it off. We're winners; we'll be fine.' That was always the pronoun: 'we.' We were a team."

Julianna couldn't stand to hear how her mother kept believing that Rory and Cade would return and bail her out—literally—and bear the burden of punishment.

Julianna did not find reports of major theft shocking anymore, maybe because there were so many famous companies and big partnerships—men, and less often, women—that did exactly what Rory and Cade had done. What was shocking, and would always be shocking, was that the Lymans had left Murielle behind.

At least Julianna had had her father and her brother, all four grandparents, good neighbors and a generous church. "Mom, would Murielle have had money of her own?"

Julianna finished creaming the sugar with the butter. She began sifting in the dry ingredients. Aiden watched eagerly.

"Yes," said her mother. "They had college accounts and investments for her. The apartment in New York was in her name."

"So she'd be rich even though everything in Rory and Cade's name was confiscated."

"The college account would still be hers, because they contributed to that from the day she was born. It didn't exist in order to hide stolen money. But the New York apartment—oh, it was huge and beautiful, just a great address!—they put it in Murielle's name to protect it. It was seized along with the yacht they never sailed and the cars they never drove and the kayaks that never went in the water. They never took vacations. It was one of the things the auditors spotted. When two partners handle huge sums of money and neither one ever takes a vacation, and when one is away, the other is always still in the office, it means you don't dare let anybody else see what you're doing."

Julianna's phone rang. She walked into the living room to get her phone out of her purse.

It was Ava. The research pit bull was going to take her first bite. Julianna wanted to weep. Instead, she said in a hard voice, "Hello, Ava."

"Hi, Julianna. Guess what? Meg and I think Cathy really is Murielle. We took pictures when you were pointing out Tommy's parents. My photo shows Cathy laughing from all the stares and Meg's picture shows Cathy shocked from all the stares. I'm sending them both to you because everybody says your mom knew Cade and Rory better than anybody. Show the pictures to your mother. If there's a resemblance, she'll see it."

Cathy did not want Mrs. Tartaglia to call her parents. She wanted the possible double to stay in Greenwich. "That's so nice of you, Mrs. Tartaglia. But I'm more worried about Latin." A stream of air-conditioning froze Cathy's arms and legs. She couldn't wait to get out of the car. It was as much of a cage as school.

Spencer wound himself around the edge of the front seat and leaned as close to Cathy in back as his seat belt would allow. "Cathy, you are amazing. I can't think about anything else, and I'm not the possible double."

She had to laugh. He was cute, even though his ridiculous hair made it hard to tell front from back.

Mrs. Tartaglia called the beauty salon on her car phone to say she was running late.

In Cathy's opinion, the person who needed the haircut was Spencer. She repressed an urge to lift his locks, as if he were a sheepdog, and find his eyes underneath.

"Yes, it is a big deal to drive from Wilton to Greenwich twice each day," Mrs. Tartaglia said to the receptionist, "but my son is very very very bright, you know."

Spencer winced. He had confessed to Cathy last week that taking Arabic wasn't his idea. He had lined up a summer job with a construction company, hoping to spend all day every day outdoors. His parents had had other plans. "What happens when I don't turn out to be quite that bright?" he murmured.

"She'll blame the teacher," Cathy comforted him, while Mrs. Tartaglia discussed hair schedules.

He nodded. "She always does. I'm never sure what to do about that, so I don't do anything. Want to hear my theory about Murielle?" He didn't wait for an answer. "My theory is the parents did come for her. After all, the parents must have known months ahead of time that they were under investigation. I bet they stashed money somewhere. I think the Cayman Islands have the banks of choice for your major-league lawless types. Next, I assume the Lymans bought fake passports. Not that I would know how to do that. But thieves find thieves, right? So here's

54

my theory: They flew out of the country as themselves and then flew right back that very minute into the U.S. under false names. International police would search where their plane landed and where their rental car got dumped, but the Lymans would already be in Atlanta, or wherever. I bet Murielle was on the phone to them the whole time. So they waited until the attention died down and then drove up to the foster home, Murielle hopped in their car and off they went to live happily ever after under aliases."

Cathy considered this. "Wouldn't there be a fuss? Wouldn't the foster parents call the police? Wouldn't the social worker mention she's down one kid? I think your theory is a little weak."

"Like my grip on Arabic. If I transfer to Latin, would it be easier?"

"Yes. Latin uses the alphabet. But you'd have missed seven days times six hours of class times three hours of homework, plus the weekend. It's actually taking me four or five hours each night. How would you catch up?"

"I'm very very very bright, you know."

Cathy laughed.

Mrs. Tartaglia exited the parkway and zipped into the commuter lot. "I don't like dropping you here, Cathy. It's a bit shabby."

"It's fine, Mrs. Tartaglia. It's not a long walk to my street. Thanks for the ride. See you tomorrow morning. Bye, Spencer." She slammed the door.

Her heart felt like a school of bluefish leaping in the water, stabbing the surface of her memory.

———

Ava usually spent Wednesday evening at her mother's, but she called to see if she could have dinner at Dad's. "Sure," said her stepmother, Kay. "Shall I pick you up? What do you want to eat?"

"I'm still a vegetarian," Ava said, because this was an ongoing collision. "Tell Dad I have a million questions."

"The Lyman case you texted about? He's been researching it all afternoon."

"He didn't know about it before?"

"Everybody knew about it before. Even I knew about it before."

Kay never followed the news. Her theory was that everybody else was following the news, so she could do something else. "All I remember," said her stepmother, "is that the Petraks could not explain a one-million-dollar deposit in their accounts. That was a bunch of money for a woman who worked part-time in a gift shop and a man who taught math at the Stamford branch of UConn."

At dinner, while her father and Kay had salmon, Ava had salad and rice. Her father said, "I didn't know there was a kid, but now that I do, I bet the million-dollar deposit was either pay for getting the kid to Europe or pay for keeping the kid in Connecticut."

"Then they didn't earn their pay," observed Ava. "Did they get to keep the million?"

"They begged the feds to take it back. They had to. Every minute that money sat in their names was another nail in their coffin. I think it went to help repay clients of the Lymans. It wouldn't have made a dent. The Lyman misrepresentations were a precipitating factor in that huge stock market decline."

56

"How did the feds know that Rory and Cade Lyman were doing anything wrong?"

"The firm couldn't pay out when clients asked for their money. Suppose you had entrusted all your savings to the Lymans. Now you want to buy a house. No problem. You have a down payment tucked away. You call Cade Lyman, and he says, 'Maybe next month.' You shout, 'It's my money—give it to me!' And he says, 'I don't have it.' Now what do you do? You're furious and you're helpless. You don't want the Lymans arrested and sent to prison, though. You'd never get your money back. To force them to pay up, you start a civil lawsuit. You're not trying to send anybody to jail, you're trying to recover your money. By the time there were half a dozen civil suits against the Lymans, the feds noticed. Usually an investigation into this kind of situation takes years. People negotiate over what papers to show the feds, and their lawyers do this, that and the next thing. Probably when the feds descended on the Lymans, it was just round one, not an arrest. Either Rory and Cade Lyman panicked, leaped on a plane and hoped for the best, or they had been planning this all along and they were ready to run. It's rare to succeed in vanishing. That's why people believed Rory and Cade made preparations to escape."

Ava nibbled a lettuce leaf. "Would Rory and Cade Lyman have done business on the Internet?"

"I'm sure they used the Internet constantly. Just like everybody else."

"So wherever they are, they're still using the Internet. They could still be reading the *Greenwich Time,* whether they're in France or Morocco or Kansas."

"It's probably their lifeline. Can you imagine the isolation they've created? What's for dessert, honey?" he asked Kay. "I'm in a dessert mood. Don't tell me how many calories anything has, just bring it on." He turned back to his daughter. "What a coincidence that Julianna Benner would be in the same class as this possible daughter."

"Who's Julianna Benner?" asked Kay.

"Julianna's mother was the Lymans' office manager. Nancy Benner went to prison for her role in what the Lymans did."

Ava choked on a half inch of lettuce.

"Ask your mom," Ava had said, as if Julianna's mother were any old mother and the Benners' situation were any old situation.

She doesn't know, thought Julianna. She didn't research that far. Do other people know? Or is Mom's role just history now?

For years, Julianna's back had been stiff, her chin high, her voice sharp. But after she said good-bye to Ava on the phone, it didn't take as much energy to stay upright. She felt a slump coming on and it was wonderful. Julianna had not slouched since the day her mother was charged with crimes.

What a gift.

It wouldn't last. Ava was on a roll and Meg was on the team. Soon they'd find the right site and the full story. Tomorrow Ava would be too embarrassed even to look at Julianna. There would be no funny foursome of Ava, Meg, Julianna and Cathy.

Julianna regretted giving Cathy the evil eye. It wasn't Cathy's fault. Even if she was Murielle, it wasn't her fault.

Julianna studied the pictures Ava had sent. In the laughing photograph, Cathy had a charming, in fact captivating, smile. Her shiny dark hair was pulled into a long careless ponytail. Her eyes danced with energy. But in the other photo, taken when Julianna named Tommy's mother and father, Cathy was a deer trapped on the highway, about to be crushed. Why was she so shaken?

Was she, in fact, Murielle?

It didn't seem logical. If Cathy was Murielle, why not admit it? If Murielle wanted to keep her identity a secret, why show up in the town where her parents were notorious and her cousin still lived? If Murielle wanted to see her aunt and uncle, all she had to do was phone. If Murielle wanted to check out the old home place, all she had to do was get in a car. Besides, accelerated Latin seemed like a tough way to sneak in and look around.

Julianna took two steps to the family computer, always on and always convenient in this tiny apartment. She Googled Norwalk High. They did offer Latin. So there was a valid reason to take this accelerated class: Cathy would be ahead one year and could start second-year Latin in the fall at her own high school. But if she was Murielle, and desperate to study Latin (did people actually get desperate to study Latin?), she could just wait a few months and safely take it at Norwalk High. Then she wouldn't risk running into a relative.

On the other hand, when your parent had done a

terrible thing and the world was watching, you had some funny reactions.

She herself was letting high school happen around her, while her heart and body stretched toward college. She hated living in Greenwich, forced to face her history every day. But no matter how many extra credits she got with accelerated Latin, no matter how high her grades, Julianna could not go away to college. She had to attend the two-year branch of the University of Connecticut (where, maddeningly, Tommy's father was a professor) and continue living in this tiny apartment, because her parents could not scrape together a nickel.

They were still paying off the lawyers. Julianna supposed the legal fees were worth it, because the prosecution had asked for a ten-year sentence and her mother's team had gotten it down to three. Nancy Benner got out in two because of good behavior. Julianna sometimes looked at her angry depressed mother and wondered what the good part had been.

Nancy Benner had been a beautiful woman. She had lost her beauty. Where had it gone in only two years? She had been a party girl, always having people over and laughing with them and telling great stories. Gone, all of it gone.

And when you went to prison for manipulating client money, you were not going to land a management position after you got out. An immense bread bakery was only a few miles away, and Mom was lucky to be hired as an ordinary hourly worker. She ran a machine in a huge windowless space that she described as prison with a nice fresh-bread smell.

Should Julianna show her mother pictures of Cathy? Ask if Mom recognized Rory or Cade in that smile?

From the kitchen, her brother called, "The oven's hot enough, Jule."

We're all in an oven, thought Julianna. And just when I thought the heat was off, Tommy Petrak turned it back on.

· 8 ·

Murielle

The man talked to Murielle as if he thought she was a puppy, or maybe a duck in need of bread crumbs. "Hi, Muffin! It's me, Matt. We're all friends here. And you know what? We're all a little worried about Mom and Dad."

Murielle said nothing. She lay on her tummy on the bedspread, resting on her elbows, while the book she had snatched up slowly flipped itself closed. She watched Matt Keefer pace. She did not want him close to the windows, maybe staring at a phone in a gutter. She did not want him noticing a new backpack. She slid off the bed and edged past him to the door.

What was in the new backpack, anyway? She had not examined it. It would not have her passport; Daddy would have that. Which meant her passport had flown to England with him. So even if she could get to the airport by herself, and even if Daddy arranged an e-ticket and even if she looked old enough to travel alone to England, they would not let her through the gates.

Murielle wanted to burst out of the house and run all the way to North Greenwich to her own house. She would be safe inside, surrounded by things that were Mommy and Daddy's. But instead, she walked quietly downstairs and Matt Keefer had to follow her. She went into the living room to be near Aunt Lois and Uncle Travis, even though it was their fault everything had gone wrong.

Two agents sat on the sofa. One sat in an armchair. Aunt Lois perched on a wooden side chair. Uncle Travis wandered. Matt Keefer followed Murielle in.

The woman agent patted the flowered upholstery next to her and said, "Want to sit here on the couch with me, Muriel?"

Murielle stopped where she was.

"How were you supposed to get to the airport, Muriel? Since your dad had your ticket? Where were you supposed to meet him?"

The living room featured a braided rug in several colors of green. Murielle preferred the deep lush pile of the carpet at her house. She dug her toe into a braid and tried to separate it.

"This is scary, isn't it?" said the woman sympathetically. "Of course you're wondering where your parents are and when they'll come get you. And we need to know too. We know they've landed in England because there's a video of them renting a car. We know they're fine because they're laughing. But what we don't know is how to talk to them or where they went in the rental car. They're not answering their cell phones. We need your help."

Murielle pretended that Aunt Lois had dropped her at

the departure gate after all, and she and Daddy waved good-bye and hurried in to catch their flight. They always flew first-class, and Daddy always bought her a present at an airport shop first. She usually chose some soft plush stuffed animal.

But she was distracted by cell phone worries. What if she couldn't reach down to the gutter? What if she reached too far and fell out the window and fell to the ground and died?

She was shaking. It had not happened to her before— her body moving without her permission. She watched it happen. The agents watched it happen. Aunt Lois tried to hug her, but Murielle turned her back on Aunt Lois.

"She's terrified! This is your fault," snapped Aunt Lois at the agents.

It's your fault, thought Murielle. If you had taken me to the airport, this wouldn't be happening.

But what was happening? What did they mean about her parents?

After a long time, Uncle Travis took Murielle into the kitchen and fixed macaroni and cheese for lunch. Murielle's absolute favorite food in the entire world was macaroni and cheese. But she could not look at it, never mind eat it.

Uncle Travis nuked leftover Thai food for himself. The spices were strong. Murielle's stomach hurt enough that she probably had appendicitis. Maybe the appendix would burst. Maybe she would go to the hospital. Then how would she get the phone?

She threw up on the floor.

————

Aunt Lois had just gotten it cleaned up when the house-keeper arrived. Mrs. Garcia had been with the Lymans for a couple of years now. She was small and round and calm. "I will take Murielle home now?" she asked. Her heavy accent had a pleasing lilt, and Murielle was glad to see her. But Murielle was going nowhere without the cell phone. Murielle did not even say hi to Mrs. Garcia. If she spoke one syllable, she'd throw up again.

Murielle wanted to run screaming for the cell phone and call Mommy and Daddy, and listen to their warm and wonderful voices, and they would explain everything and solve it, and above all, they would come.

Her arms were too short to reach way down to the gutter. She would need something long to poke the phone with. Maybe a yardstick or an umbrella. She'd flip the phone out of the gutter and onto the grass.

Mrs. Garcia left.

The agents left.

The hours passed. Tommy came home from school and offered to play video games with her—anything she wanted—but the only thing she wanted was her cell phone. During dinner she sat silently on a kitchen chair and tried to reach her parents by thought waves. Come. Come now.

Eventually it was night.

Aunt Lois coaxed Murielle into warm pajamas, her favorite navy blue flannels with the white dots, even though it was June and the night was warm enough for shortie pajamas. She wrapped Murielle in the pink fluffy robe, and Murielle had a moment of panic, because the new backpack was fully exposed, but Aunt Lois did not notice. Murielle always had new everything. Aunt Lois wouldn't question a new backpack, even on practically the last day of the school year.

Murielle lay in bed, watching the luminous dial on the little bedside clock. When it seemed safe, she tiptoed downstairs and dug around in the coat closet until she found the cane Uncle Travis had used the year after he'd had foot surgery. Back in her room, she opened the window as far as it would go. It made noise but not enough to alert anybody.

The white gutter glinted in the moonlight. She could see a little dark patch that was the phone. She leaned way out of the window, steering the cane down into the gutter. When it touched the phone, she tried to drive it out, like a golfer whose ball had landed in sand.

She tried once.

Twice.

The third time, she hit the phone good and hard and it flew forward.

But it did not sail out onto the grass.

It shot down the gutter like a bowling ball and fell into the downspout.

After the first horror, she thought, It's okay. It'll fall straight down. The downspout has that little curve at the bottom. I'll stick my hand up and get it.

She did not put on the fluffy pink robe, which would be visible in the moonlight, but headed outside in the navy blue pajamas.

There was no alarm system to disable. At her own house, even opening a window meant entering a code in the control panel. Here she simply turned the bolt in the side door and stepped out. Two concrete steps and she was barefoot in the grass. It was wet, which startled her, and made her think of slimy things.

The neighbors' dog barked.

She didn't dare call to reassure the dog because everybody's windows were open.

Normally Murielle did not like the dark and would not dream of being outside in it. In spite of how many houses were crammed together, this area was wooded, full of deer and raccoons. Turkeys raided bird feeders and skunks turned the garbage over. Murielle liked the environment and watched Animal Planet all the time, but that didn't mean she wanted to crawl around the yard after midnight and maybe encounter an actual animal.

She could not remember what time it would be in England right now. But if Mommy and Daddy were asleep, they would not mind waking up for her.

The downspout was hidden by overgrown shrubs. Murielle knelt down and parted the bushes to find the white cylinder. She patted the ground in case the cell phone had been flung all the way out, like a toddler coming down a slide. She found nothing. She stuck her hand in the downspout and found a handful of leaves, wet and smelly. Bravely she stuck her hand deeper into the tube, extricating gobs of leaves. She could reach no farther, because the downspout turned upward and ran up the side of the house to meet the gutter below her bedroom window.

Aunt Lois and Uncle Travis had not cleaned the gutters in a long time. Murielle's cell phone was stuck somewhere in the middle.

Even then she stayed calm. Gutters came in sections

that were rammed into each other and held against the house with little straps. In the morning, Murielle would find a screwdriver, unfasten the straps and pull on the gutter bottom until she got rid of the curved piece, and maybe the next piece too, and she'd use a rake handle to clear the rest of the dead leaves and she'd find her cell phone.

She backed out of the shrubbery. She was filthy and soaking wet. She wanted her parents. She wanted to cry. She sat on the cold concrete step at the side door and stared at the moon and the stars. The man who delivered the newspaper at five a.m. saw her lying there and called the police.

By the time Murielle was fully awake, police cars were parked in the driveway. Lights whirled. Two of the initials people were back. Neighbors had come out. Aunt Lois was still in her nightgown, which was a huge old T-shirt, and looked awful.

"You didn't know that your niece slept outside all night?" demanded the police.

Aunt Lois was stunned. "No," she whispered.

"You didn't check on her?" they said, voices loaded with disgust.

Aunt Lois tried to ignore them. "Muffin, honey, what happened? What are you doing out here?"

Murielle wanted a hug and a shower and fresh clothing. She wanted her aunt. But if she said a single word, she might accidentally release a clue about her precious cell phone. She was a partner. There were secrets to keep.

"She's covered with dirt and leaves," said the policeman. "Honey, were you trying to run away and you fell down but you managed to get back here? Something like that?"

Murielle had never once thought of running away. Daddy had said that they were coming for her, so whether she managed a phone call or not, she had to stay here, and wait.

She shivered in her navy blue pajamas and stayed silent.

And then they were all back in the house again, except the neighbors, and Aunt Lois was sobbing and Uncle Travis was swearing and even Cousin Tommy was yelling at the police and the initials people to get out of their house and leave them alone.

They let Aunt Lois take Murielle upstairs, and get her in the shower, and help with her shampoo, and blow her hair dry, and get her into clean clothes, during which both Murielle and Aunt Lois sobbed steadily.

And then they were back in the living room and Murielle was seated on the sofa. She was small enough that her feet dangled when she sat all the way back. She felt like a three-year-old. She reminded herself that she was ten and her parents' partner in keeping secrets. On the coffee table in front of her, a tray of snacks had been placed, in case Murielle decided to eat. The table was glass and had not recently been cleaned. Smudgy fingerprints reflected the sunlight. They weren't Mommy's or Daddy's. They were almost never in this room.

Matt Keefer hitched over a plain wooden chair, one of a pair that sat against the far wall on either side of a narrow table that held dried flowers in a bowl. The flowers were dusty. He sat backward on the chair, riding it like a motorcycle. "Muriel, we're really worried about your mother and father. Can you tell us how to reach them?"

Murielle could not imagine worrying about her parents. They were strong and tough. They shrugged at any problem. "We'll deal," they would say. Furthermore, her parents had caught their planes. They were exactly where they'd planned to be, which was always the case.

Now her cousin Tommy sat down beside her. She adored Tommy. She looked at him, grateful and expectant. But he was mad at her. He was twitchy and frantic. He drilled her with his words. "Muffin. Aunt Rory and Uncle Cade have done bad stuff. They stole money. They stole a lot of money. We have to find them, because these people are trying to blame my mom and dad as well. And my mom and dad don't have anything to do with what Aunt Rory and Uncle Cade did." Tommy's voice turned fierce. His face got too close to hers. "You tell this policeman how to reach Rory and Cade. You tell him now!"

Her parents would never steal. She hated Tommy. She would tell Tommy what she thought of him. She opened her mouth. I'll never tell you! she would shout. I'm the only one who can reach them! I have a special phone Daddy gave me just in case.

She clamped her jaws. She swallowed her words.

The grown-ups leaned closer, like growing plants. Their heads waved around, faces on stalks.

Out in the hallway, one of them said to Uncle Travis, "We've set up an office in the Lymans' house."

Murielle's house? Her real house?

Her parents would never want these people in their home. Murielle knew from television shows that police had to have special permission from judges just to get in the door, never mind stay there. What would they do inside her house? What could they want?

She remembered suddenly that her parents had been home every night last week, although way too busy to watch TV with Murielle. They had been shredding. Everybody's parents had a shredder to chop up bank and brokerage statements. Kelsey used her parents' shredded papers for the hamsters. Last week, Mommy and Daddy had stuffed their shredded paper into black plastic garbage bags and loaded them into their cars. Her parents were the least likely people in the world to handle their own garbage. They didn't even take their cars to the dealership for oil changes. The dealer came to them instead. And now Mommy and Daddy were making trash runs?

Her father had laughed. "We're distributing it evenly throughout the area."

It didn't matter what had been written on that paper, because it was shredded and by now the trash would have been picked up. But there were still the computers, with the original information. Mommy and Daddy had their laptops with them, of course. But the desktop computers? What would be in them?

The woman initials person sat down between Murielle and her cousin, and put an arm around Murielle. Murielle sat like a Barbie doll bent into sitting position. She pretended the woman's arm wasn't there.

Out in the hall her aunt and uncle were being offered

something called immunity. She knew the word from getting shots at a doctor's. There was a little jab that did hurt and after that, you couldn't be hurt, at least not by that disease. She couldn't get the meaning of the word as the agents were using it. The feds, Tommy was calling them.

The woman said, "Sweetie, I know you feel sad. It's awful to be abandoned by your parents."

Abandoned?

Like an unwanted pet?

Murielle Lyman wrapped her arms around herself so her heart didn't fall out. She had not been abandoned. She was sitting here because of Aunt Lois, not because of her parents. And Murielle had talked to Daddy. He was coming for her.

Murielle opened her mouth to make a case for Daddy. Just in time, she stopped herself. They were clever, these initials people, and she was not. She had to make a rule: no talking. That would always work.

People came and went.

And suddenly the initials people were saying, "Muriel, you're going to spend the night with some new friends while we keep talking to your aunt and uncle. This is Mrs. O'Neill. She's from the Department of Children and Families, and she'll get you all settled in. It's for a very very short time, until things get straightened out."

Not without my phone! she almost screamed.

Uncle Travis raised his voice. "You can't do this. I've called our lawyer. He's on the way. You have to wait for him. You leave our niece here!"

"Muriel needs a safe place for a few days. It's our job to provide one."

"She's safe here!" snapped Aunt Lois. "She belongs with us! Don't you dare take her."

"Your sister put a million dollars in your account, Mrs. Petrak," said the agent, enunciating it carefully: "uh ... mill ... yun."

"I didn't ask her to!"

"You are part of this scam. You knew Rory and Cade were flying separately from different airports, in the hope that their flights would look like ordinary business trips and nobody would notice or stop them. Your job was to bring the daughter. You knew Cade Lyman had Muriel's passport with him. You knew they were trying to get out of the country and avoid arrest."

"I did not. They were always flying here and there. I didn't think about passports. I didn't know their destination. They could have been going to their country place. Murielle didn't even have a bag to check."

"Where's their country place?"

"A little ranch in Wyoming. They don't take luggage because they keep full wardrobes hanging in the closets waiting for them."

"You don't fly to Wyoming from an international gate, and your note to yourself—which we found in your car—lists an international gate."

Mrs. O'Neill took Murielle's hand and led her upstairs to pack some clothes. Aunt Lois ran after them, shouting, "You can't do this!"

In the bedroom, Mrs. O'Neill put clothes into a bag while Aunt Lois tried to take the clothes back out. Murielle eased over to the closet door, took her new backpack off the hook and slid it onto her shoulders.

"You ready, honey?" said the lady named O'Neill.

"You cannot take her away!" shouted Aunt Lois. "She's upset! We're all upset! But—"

"It's for the little girl's own good. She needs some counseling, a little hot food, a warm bed and better supervision. Your attitude leaves a lot to be desired. This is just for a few days, until we figure out what's happening."

Murielle was bundled into the backseat of a car. When Murielle did not fasten the seat belt, Mrs. O'Neill reached around her to snap it in place. Murielle felt as if she had been handcuffed. If they found Mommy and Daddy, would they handcuff them?

This was such a shocking image that Murielle did not glance back to wave good-bye to her aunt and uncle and cousin. Murielle did not cry. Mommy and Daddy were never impressed by crying. "Don't whine," they would say. "Just solve it."

How do I solve this? Murielle made a mental list. Stay silent. Wait for Daddy.

That was the whole list.

The woman in the front seat spoke over her shoulder. "If your parents love you, Muriel, they'll come back."

· 9 ·

Cathy

The flat cracked asphalt of the Norwalk commuter parking lot was as challenging as a balance beam. Cathy could hardly stay upright.

Nothing had gone according to plan.

She had not meant her past to leap up and hit her in the face. She had thought she could just look at her past. Stand on the sidewalk, as it were, and gaze at people and places that had meant something once.

It had not crossed her mind that Tommy would recognize her. When the exact same cousin she had seen five years ago—just taller and broader—knelt to look up into her face, she thought her body would split open and Murielle would step out.

Cathy had hung on to her chair and her brown paper bag. She could not allow Murielle to have a voice.

Five years ago, when she was little and understood nothing and was so afraid, so lonely and desperate, she had been questioned by the authorities to the point of vomiting. Even now, it plagued her dreams. In nightmares, she handed the FBI some crucial clue. They laughed: long drawn-out taunting laughs. They rubbed their hands in glee. After all these years, Rory and Cade were caught the way the animal cops caught stray dogs on TV. Metal hoops were thrust around their necks. Her mother and father were dragged by the throat and shoved into cages, where they cowered in the corner. In the worst version, people in uniform decided that Rory and Cade Lyman, like vicious animals trained for dog fights, were dangerous and must be euthanized.

She would wake up fighting the sheets and blankets, screaming silently to her parents—*I didn't turn you in! I still love you! Please come home! I meant to call! I tried my best!*

Cathy sat down on the curb between the parking lot and the sidewalk. It had crumbled from the force of weeds coming up through the cracks. How strong and persistent the thin scraggly weeds were. Like Murielle, they were going to surface no matter what the odds.

Cathy had no tissues with her. It was such a hot day she didn't even have a sleeve. She wept into her hands.

She felt like a thin-shelled egg, pecked on the inside by the sharp beak of Murielle, trying to get out.

When she had—so stupidly; so naively—planned this, Cathy had expected to spot Tommy Petrak the first day. She would have the advantage, because Tommy would be using his own name. No matter how much he might have changed from age twelve to age seventeen, she would know which boy he was when they read out the attendance list. But when he looked in *her* direction, he would see only

76

a girl named Cathy Ferris. Cathy believed that she looked pretty much like any teenage girl with long dark hair in a ponytail.

She assumed that over the course of six weeks, the topic of her classmate's aunt Rory and uncle Cade and cousin Murielle would come up. She would listen in. She would learn that crucial thing: had Rory and Cade Lyman ever come looking for their daughter? But nobody would connect her to the old scandal. She would be a kid from out of town with a weird interest in Latin, even when she asked for details from people who knew the Lyman story.

But on the first day of summer school, Cathy had been taken straight from the office to the Latin room. At lunch, the Chinese class in which Tommy was enrolled never appeared. Instead, Cathy became friends with Ava, Meg and Julianna; enjoyed Graydon, Ethan and Colton; got comfortable with Spencer and his mother; and, to her utter amazement, fell in love with Latin.

Latin, like math and music, was full of cadence and rhythm. She loved the sentence structure, which reminded her of algebra, with its orderly equations. She loved the memory work. It was as if her mind had been waiting for lists of conjugations and declensions; for vocabulary whose syllables leaped over the centuries and showed up in English.

At the moment Thomas Petrak crossed the student center to accuse her of being Murielle, she had forgotten why she was here.

There she sat in her pistachio-green chair, brainless as an amoeba, while the entire summer school climbed on board. In minutes, they were totally into the saga of

Murielle. The privacy of five years vanished. And Cathy was unable to think at all, let alone fast enough to retreat.

Everyone she knew was at ease using the Internet, but this crowd—spectacular students all—would nail every detail from every conceivable source. It would not surprise Cathy if some of her classmates already knew as much about Rory and Cade's crimes and fate as she did.

Cathy dragged herself to her feet. The summer heat reflected off the dark tar and baked what little brain she had left. She tottered home. Uphill all the way.

How could she face Julianna tomorrow morning?

Murielle had met Mrs. Benner often in that suite at the top of Greenwich Avenue, with its view downhill to Long Island Sound and the sparkling water. The view was for clients. Murielle's parents never glanced at it. Their lives were on the computer screen, where they watched the exciting landscape of money made and lost.

Murielle had never met Julianna, and maybe never heard the name, but she did remember a younger brother. Aiden had taken horseback riding at the same stable as Murielle. He must also live in this tiny apartment the Benners had only because of the kindness of others.

I didn't know her last name, thought Cathy. And if I heard it, it didn't register. I went to Greenwich thinking only of myself.

She had no recollection of the trial of Nancy Benner. It must have happened many months after Rory and Cade vanished, when Murielle had stopped going to the *Greenwich Time* Web site; stopped hoping for news. Stopped being Murielle.

Julianna was the proof Cathy had never wanted: Rory

and Cade really and truly had done terrible things, and then shrugged while their victims suffered.

She had never noticed how bad the sidewalks were, how cracked and tilted. Because I never stared at my feet before, she thought. I always look ahead, not down.

She hated her posture, full of shame and fury.

She hated Rory and Cade. She could not call them Mommy or Daddy today.

When she got into the house and set her book bag down, she had to start her chores. If she didn't do the laundry, she'd have to explain why not. Not once in all these years had they discussed her past.

She wasn't ready today, either.

In each bedroom, she threw the covers back, pulled up the sheets and peeled off the pillowcases. A metaphor for Murielle, whose cover was about to come off.

She wanted to rip the sheets to shreds. She wanted to slam her fist through the wall and chew on doorknobs. How dare you? she screamed silently at Rory and Cade. *You are my parents.* How dare you run away and never come back?

I should have grown up in Greenwich, instead of sneaking in by way of summer school. I should have had that cousin and those friends. I should have had you! You took my life away, just like you took Julianna Benner's life away.

In the laundry room, she filled the washer with sheets. She hoisted the heavy jug of liquid detergent, but a minute passed before she had enough control to pour. If she spilled, she'd only have to clean it up. Do you know how many lives you spilled? she asked her parents.

She emptied the dryer of yesterday's load, but could

not fold. Neatness was impossible. Only violence had appeal. She didn't want to curl her fingers gently around the edges of T-shirts and make the ends meet. She wanted to claw the air and slap a memory around.

That's all you are! she screamed at them. Memories! You even took away Christmas and birthdays and anniversaries. I never got to draw a card for you or make you a special present. I never got to worry about what to get you, something you would cherish and keep on the mantel or wear on your dress. You didn't cherish me. You cherished cash.

Out the tiny laundry room window, she saw Marmee's car pull into the driveway. The garage was not attached to the house, and they never used it for the cars anyway because it was their only storeroom.

She stared at her foster mother. She loved Marmee in a quiet dutiful way. She wanted to love her real mother, in a deep passionate solid safe way.

It would never happen.

What had she been thinking, getting herself to that summer school? That she could get her parents' love back by showing up in the same geographical area where they had all once lived?

In the backseat of Marmee's car, Jamesy undid his seat belt and opened the car door, two things he was not allowed to do and therefore always did. If there was a rule to break, Jamesy was all over it. She opened the kitchen door and waved at Jamesy in the hope that he'd run into the house instead of into the street.

"Hi, Cathy!" he shouted. "I'm hungry!"

Jamesy always had his priorities straight. Eat first. Perhaps she could learn from him. Her technique—eat last or not at all—was not working.

Jamesy raced past her into the kitchen and threw open the cabinet door behind which the best snacks waited. His day care passed out a fruit snack in the afternoon, but Jamesy did not think an apple was food. He ripped open a pack of miniature cookies.

When he arrived last year, he was a biter, a bed wetter, a kicker, a screamer and a spitter. Cathy could not believe anybody would volunteer to share a house with him. "Does he have a good feature?" she had asked.

"He is hard to love," agreed Marmee. "But if God can love him, so can we. Every time Jamesy hurts you or annoys you or you have to clean up after him, ask God to give you patience."

A month later, Cathy said, "We're wearing God out."

"I know. Progress: zero."

But slowly, Jamesy turned into a person. He no longer threw half-empty plates across the room and laughed when the china broke and the food spattered. Sometimes while Cathy did homework at the kitchen bar, he would color beside her, and not intentionally crayon the walls, the counter and his new shoes as well. He had never seen a picture book until he came here, and now he would even ask sort of nicely if Cathy would read to him. He liked to sit on the couch with her and snuggle under the prayer shawl somebody knit for Marmee a few years ago when she had cancer. And although Jamesy was willing to destroy almost anything almost anytime, even he understood that the church ladies had knit their prayers for Marmee's health into that wool, and that it warmed Marmee just to look at it.

Cathy had come to love Jamesy. Love was interesting. It didn't necessarily arrive on its own. You could make a decision to have it. You didn't have to start with anything.

Jamesy rushed over to her. "Want a chewy bar?" he asked, holding it out.

Jamesy did not share. He had never heard of sharing. For Jamesy to bring her one of his snacks was like being visited by the Magi and given gold. Cathy hugged him. He hugged back. Aunt Lois wanted that hug, she thought. A hug is so simple. I can hug. But I can't hug Aunt Lois. Aunt Lois wanted to turn my mother in. Aunt Lois is the enemy.

This childish belief that had kept Murielle from calling Aunt Lois felt as intense as ever. But the Aunt Lois who had held out her arms, who had called to her, who had yearned, ached, panted for her! That Aunt Lois, standing in the sun, calling her Muffin, was no enemy.

What am I going to do? Am I going to keep Cathy? I like Cathy. Cathy is safe. She doesn't get interrogated by the FBI. She doesn't betray her parents.

But oh! to be Murielle again.

She reminded herself that Murielle did not exist. The parents of Murielle did not exist. The house of Murielle belonged to others. The life of Murielle was over.

"Thank you, Jamesy. Want me to read to you?" Her throat was tight. She shouldn't have offered. She could hardly speak.

"Yes. I want to read all my books. All in a row."

Cathy was as soothed as Jamesy by the gentle rhythmic

stories, the beautiful pictures, the soft turning of pages. He fell asleep leaning on her. Day care took a lot out of a person, especially in nice weather, when the kids ran around outside all afternoon. A nap this late would make bedtime hard, though, and when you lived with a boy like Jamesy, you prayed for his bedtime to arrive early, not late.

Jamesy was heavy against her shoulder. She shifted his weight a little and tucked the prayer shawl around his shoulders.

His caseworker marveled at how well Jamesy was doing in the Ferris household. The caseworker did not seem to realize that Cathy was also a foster child. Cathy herself had not seen or heard from a caseworker in ages. The system had not lost her, because the monthly stipend for her support continued to arrive. There was no understanding bureaucracy. And in the end, the State of Connecticut had been more dependable than her mother and father.

In the kitchen Marmee and Dad Bob were arguing, which they rarely did. She turned up her iPod to drown them out and listened to the slow recitations of verbs and verb endings; of adjectives and nouns and their endings. She preferred the Latin study CD that she used on the computer. When dinner was ready, she woke Jamesy up, and he was so whiny, she asked if she could take her plate to her room and study at the computer while she ate.

Normally her parents did not allow this. Dinner together was the rule and food in a bedroom was against the rules.

She had not thought in years about dinner in the Lyman household, but today she was awash in memory. Murielle and the au pair would have whatever the housekeeper fixed. Her parents skipped meals, ate in front of their computers or went to restaurants. Sometimes they weren't home until long after Murielle was fast asleep. Sometimes they left in the morning before Murielle was awake.

"Sure," said Dad Bob. "I know how much homework you have."

In her room, she submerged herself in Latin. Submerge: from *sub*, "under," and *mergere*, "to plunge." Every now and then, she paused just to read the Latin dictionary in the back of her Wheelock. The vocabulary in this chapter was especially good. *Nox, noctis*—"night." As in "nocturnal" and "equinox." She looked up "equinox" in her online encyclopedia. A night and day of equal length all over the world. There were a vernal—spring—and an autumnal equinox. Twice a year, no matter where Rory and Cade lived, they shared something with their daughter. Sunlight and shadow.

How ephemeral. How meaningless. How sad.

Marmee poked her head in. "Come say good night to Jamesy."

Cathy pulled herself together, went into Jamesy's room and flopped down on the bed next to him. "Sleep tight, bunny rabbit."

He loved this game. "I'm not a bunny."

"Oh. Sleep tight, tiger."

"I'm not a tiger."

"Oh. Sleep tight, potato chip."

"I'm not a potato chip!"

"Oh. What are you, then?"

"No, no, don't stop yet. Keep telling me to sleep tight."

"Sleep tight, beach ball."

Marmee and Dad went back downstairs, leaving her to finish the long bedtime ritual and get Jamesy to sleep. This was unusual. They liked Jamesy to know that his foster parents were there when night came and they'd be there when morning came.

The first rule of being a parent, thought Cathy. You have to be home.

The terrible anger at parents who had decided never to come home threaded its way through every capillary of her being.

But it did not tell her what to do in the morning.

· 10 ·

Murielle

It seemed to Murielle that the social worker drove forever to arrive at the place where Murielle would spend the night. It was a small house, much smaller than her own house, and even smaller than Kelsey's or Aunt Lois's. Mrs. O'Neill led Murielle inside. It smelled funny and was packed with strangers.

"This is Muriel," said Mrs. O'Neill, thus ensuring that nobody would ever pronounce her name right. "She's ten and she's having a hard time eating and sleeping because of family problems."

Murielle did not have family problems. Her problem was Aunt Lois, who had not let her travel with her family.

"This is your foster home, sweetheart," Mrs. O'Neill told her. "I'll be back to check on you, but I know you're going to be fine."

Murielle had never heard of a foster home. She did not even know what the word "foster" meant. She started to protest that this was just for one night; Mrs. O'Neill had specifically said that; and now it sounded— But Mrs. O'Neill was gone.

In the morning, the foster father went to work and the foster mother did laundry. There were three other foster children: Raphael, Latisha and Luke. They had nothing to do all day because the school year was over. They watched television, played in the small fenced backyard and listened to music. Since Murielle didn't talk, Raphael, Latisha and Luke talked for her, around her and about her.

"Lunchtime," said the foster mother. "Let's all pitch in."

Murielle had never "pitched in" in her life. She had no chores. Neither did her parents. The housekeeper, the maid service and the landscapers did everything.

Latisha refused to do a thing. The foster mother insisted. Latisha didn't care how she behaved. She just wanted to get her way. When she didn't, she sobbed. She made as much noise as she could. She didn't use a tissue. When the foster mother tried to pull her off the floor, Latisha curled into a ball.

The foster mother gave in. Latisha didn't have to help. Murielle was impressed.

For supper there was a huge tuna noodle casserole, in a baking dish of a size Murielle had only ever seen at church suppers. She had never liked the smell of tuna. She didn't like it now, either. Anyway, she couldn't lift her hands off her lap to hold a fork. She didn't eat a thing. But afterward, she didn't mind helping, the way Latisha minded. It was something to do.

The foster mother thought it was very funny that Murielle had to be taught how to wash and dry dishes. "They must have had a dishwasher," said the foster mother.

"Wish we could afford one," said the father glumly.

There had never been occasion in Murielle's life to use that sentence.

After supper, the father turned on the television news. The big story was about a Wall Street husband-and-wife team, bad people named Rory and Cade Lyman. They had invested a lot of money for a lot of people, but lost most of the money taking a position in natural gas. They could not give their clients back their money. Not even some of it. This caught the attention of the SEC and the NASD. The reporter did not say what the initials stood for.

Airport surveillance video caught Rory and Cade Lyman getting off their separate planes in London. It also filmed them together at the rental car counter. Where they were handing over credit cards and high-fiving each other.

Murielle stared at the grainy black-and-white stills of her mother and father. She should have been there too, celebrating!

But what was there to celebrate?

"No trace of them has been found," said the reporter. "But their pictures are being circulated. They are probably using false names and false passports."

A British policeman with a charming accent expected to capture the Lymans shortly and return them to America.

"Capture." Another animal-cops word, like "abandoned." When you captured a stray animal, you caged it.

Her mother and father.

Nobody in the small busy house glanced at Murielle, who wasn't mentioned in the news report. The social worker had not used her last name when she brought Murielle here, though it was undoubtedly in the pack of papers handed to the foster mother. But the foster mother did not have time for paperwork. The file lay on a shelf and was already under a layer of other stuff.

Muriel, they kept saying. Muriel this, Muriel that.

That night she shared a bedroom with Latisha, who didn't like anything in the world, let alone Murielle. Murielle admired Latisha. Why hadn't Murielle screamed and stomped? What was she doing here? How could she get home? How were Mommy and Daddy going to find her here? What if the police found them first? And how would they get across the ocean now that the British police were looking at everybody who got on a plane?

Mrs. O'Neill showed up the next day. "How's Muriel doing?"

"She's hardly eaten a scrap of food. Look how thin she is."

They all looked at how thin she was.

"What's her situation?" asked the foster mother.

"She has an aunt and uncle. But they're being investigated as accessories. If they're not indicted, we'll probably return her. Meantime, we've done a TPR."

Mrs. O'Neill probably thought Murielle wouldn't know what that meant. But Latisha, Raphael and Luke had talked. A TPR had happened to Raphael. It stood for Termination of Parental Rights. It meant Connecticut decided that your mother and father could never have you again.

A TPR.

On Murielle Lyman.

The State of Connecticut thought Mommy and Daddy were such bad people that Murielle could not even live with them.

Murielle was dazed. Her parents were wonderful!

Mrs. O'Neill left. The volume on the television was turned back up. Ice cream sandwiches were served. The television news said that Rory and Cade Lyman had not yet been captured. They had ruined the lives and futures of their clients and employees, and must be found.

"Next week," said the foster mother to the four children, "you'll all go to new families. We do only short-term stays, and in July, we always go camping." She beamed. "We've got reservations at state parks. We'll fish and swim and picnic and lie around."

"Ugh," said Latisha. "Mosquitoes. I wouldn't go with you anyway."

"I can fish," said Luke, who always claimed to have done everything and be good at it. "I'm a good swimmer. I camp all the time. Can I go?"

"Can I go too?" asked Raphael. "I'll be good. I've never gone fishing."

Raphael could not go home because there wasn't one. His father was unknown, his mother was in jail and his grandmother had given up.

"No," said the foster mother briskly. "Don't worry, Raphael. You'll have a lovely new family."

Don't worry?

Murielle thought it was absolutely amazing that anybody could look Raphael in the eye and tell him not to worry.

Raphael went outside to play. He lay on the grass driving tiny metal trucks through thickets of dry grass and over bridges of twigs. Murielle sat down beside him. He was tough and angry and she was afraid of him, but she liked him. "Raphael? What happens to grown-ups who steal money?"

"They go to prison. Like my mom. Why?"

"It isn't true, but people think my parents stole money."

Raphael shook his head. "They don't put you in foster care for nothing. If you're here, then they stole it."

After that, Murielle couldn't even sit at the kitchen table, let alone eat.

Mrs. O'Neill took her to a pediatrician.

"Hi, Muriel," said the doctor, not bothering to leaf through the folder Mrs. O'Neill had handed her. "So you don't want to eat. Tell me why not."

If your parents love you, they'll come back.

Murielle closed her eyes to keep her thoughts inside and tightened her lips to keep her speech inside. Her parents did love her. They were coming back. She could deal, like her parents. Mommy and Daddy would be here soon.

The pediatrician said, "Sometimes when kids can't eat, they can drink. See if she'll have a milk shake. Take her to Friendly's down the street. If that works, bring her back and we'll figure out a liquid diet for a few days and maybe get her jump-started."

The waitress at Friendly's was old and fat and gray and tired.

Murielle didn't order. Mrs. O'Neill was irritated. The waitress said, "Nice thing about our menu, it's full of pictures. You just point at the best picture, sweet pea, and I'll bring it."

Murielle tapped the picture of the chocolate sundae,

and when it came, it was not too large and it was not too small, and when Murielle had a spoonful, the rich vanilla ice cream and the hot sticky chocolate slid effortlessly down her throat.

"Thank you," she said to the waitress when they left.

At the pediatrician's, the social worker took all the credit.

The pediatrician wrote out a prescription. "Best," she said to Murielle, "is to eat regular food. But if you feel sick and icky, drink this. It's a fortified chocolate milk shake. Are you going to do this for me, Muriel?" The pediatrician was scribbling in the medical folder. The folder was green, and the label was narrow and white. Typed on the label was: Lyman, Murielle Catherine.

Only kids with really popular first names used their middle names too. In her fourth grade were two Jadens and two Aidens, three Emilys and two Madisons. They often used their middle names. To be different from Emily Elizabeth and Emily Arianna, Emily Quinn had begun dropping the Emily and calling herself Quinn.

There was only one Murielle, so she had never needed her middle name.

"Muriel?" said the pediatrician. "I need an answer, honey."

She could not seem to correct people when they said "Muriel." And she didn't want to be "Murielle" now; she would save that for Mommy and Daddy. They would be here soon. She knew it. They would tell the State of Connecticut what they could do with their TPR. Because they did love their daughter. So there.

The waitress at Friendly's had used pictures. Murielle

used the label. She pointed. "I use my middle name," she whispered, tapping "Catherine." Her first speech in days was a lie.

"Hey, great!" The doctor grinned. " 'Cathy'! I love that name. 'Muriel' is kind of dumpy, isn't it? Cathy, I'm going to see you next week. I want you to chow down like a regular kid, okay?"

But she was not a regular kid. She was a foster child. That very afternoon she found herself on her way to her second home. "I'm Veronica. I'm your caseworker now, Muriel," said a different woman.

Murielle was a case. Not a daughter, not a fourth grader, not a niece, not a friend. A case.

"It turns out that her name is Cathy," said the first foster mother.

The social worker made a note of this and reached for Murielle's hand to take her away. Murielle gave Raphael and Latisha and Luke a terrified look, and Latisha said, "It's not so bad. You'll be okay."

"If I can do it, you can do it," said Raphael.

"It's better if you talk," Luke told her. "Talk to the next people."

At the second home, her caseworker introduced her as Cathy.

"Cathy" turned out to be a pleasant name that demanded nothing. On TV, the news claimed that her mother and father were using false names. Me too, she thought, proud of herself.

That night it rained. Torrential pounding rain, with rolls of thunder and explosions of lightning. Murielle had never considered rain. At Aunt Lois's house, this rain would stream down the roof and into the gutter and it would fill the spout. It would drown the phone. The phone would never work again. There was no way now to call her mother and father.

Every decision Murielle had made was wrong.

The voice of Mrs. O'Neill played in her head: if your mother and father love you, they'll come back.

But they didn't come.

· 11 ·

Cathy

She woke during the night.

The Ferris house was close to the road, and there was nearly always traffic. Headlights from passing cars shone through the window and rushed around the walls. She did not pull the blinds down, but watched the pulse of invisible traffic.

She, with her invisible parents.

After a long time, she got up and went to her closet. Her bare feet were soundless on the carpet. Hanging in the back, shoulder straps twisted around a wooden hanger, was a small child's backpack. She took it down and held it for a while, as if it were a teddy bear or a blankie. Then she turned on the bedside lamp, and for the first time in years, looked through the contents.

There was a hoodie, knit from soft fluffy wool, with a small pack of tissues tucked in the front left pocket. There was a paperback she had read many times, her favorite in the Laura Ingalls Wilder Little House series. There was a little snap-top leather change purse with some change. There was an inside zip pocket where once upon a time there had been ten one-hundred-dollar bills.

She had often puzzled about those bills. What had her parents envisioned? That at age ten she might need to pay for hotel rooms or dinner?

Her parents had lost home, jobs, country and daughter all at once.

Her brilliant excitable energetic parents, stranded with nothing. Well, money. They had money.

But how could they risk even a simple shopping trip, never mind going to the concert or the art gallery or the fine restaurant? Were they holed up with all that money, eating cold cereal in front of daytime television? Had they gotten plastic surgery? Dyed their hair? Forced themselves to gain weight—her parents, to whom trim bodies were crucial to existence? Did they look over their shoulders, terrified of being found? Or were they sailing a yacht on some sunlit sea, with not a care in the world?

The shadow life that had always been with her seemed darker now; almost solid. Her anger had also settled down and hardened. Inside her chest, her heart felt as heavy as that jug of detergent, some awful container of acid.

A mental flicker of light interrupted her thoughts, like distant lightning. She held still, staring into the dark, waiting for another flash.

Spencer's theory: Rory and Cade had flown immediately back to the USA under fake names.

Mrs. Shaw's remark: Rory and Cade had investments and property.

"Investments," when referring to Rory and Cade,

meant stocks, bonds, margins and funds. "Property" meant their house in Greenwich, the apartment in New York, the cottage in the Hamptons and the little ranch in Wyoming.

But put the words together—"investment property"— and she could vaguely picture a tall shabby house; a triple-decker. One floor to a family, each with its tiny corner porch. She had been there once. She remembered because she wanted to stay in the car but Daddy said it wasn't a safe neighborhood and she had come inside too.

She sighed at the concept of Cade wanting her to be safe.

Oh, Daddy, she thought. Not so much, in the end.

She raked mentally through everything she knew about "investment property." Rory and Cade had been determined to make a fortune. Before they became stockbrokers, they tried being landlords and bought real estate. They had owned at least one rental. Had they kept it? Did they still own it when they came back to America to hide? Did they own it now?

If Spencer's theory was right, they had landed back in America almost before the FBI showed up at Aunt Lois's. They would have needed a place to live. A place where they would never be recognized. Where nobody would even think of them. Where people did not ski, eat at fine restaurants, own horses, belong to tennis clubs, golf at famous courses or drive expensive cars.

People living in Greenwich faced New York City. They hardly knew that Connecticut extended behind them to the east. Oh, sure, they had friends in other wealthy commuter towns, like New Canaan and Darien and Wilton.

But mentally, their capital was Manhattan, not Hartford, Connecticut. Most of them had never even been to Hartford. As for sad little cities like Willimantic and Norwich and Waterbury, with their dreary half-abandoned downtowns, large immigrant populations, mediocre housing and lack of fine shopping: they were unknown to the Greenwich resident. Why would anybody go there?

And so if Rory and Cade did go to such a town, they would never cross paths with their rich former friends. Or their ruined former clients.

Whatever the original plan, Rory and Cade had faced an immediate screwup. No Murielle. Had they decided to hang out in a grim little apartment on some grim little street, waiting for the moment they could carry out a drive-by seizure of their own baby girl?

Over the interviews, across the years, through the nightmares, even though she was terrified that she might give away a clue to her parents' whereabouts, Murielle had known that she did not have such a clue.

But maybe she did.

In the dark came chills like the onset of flu. Her body prickled and her muscles ached.

Her parents had had a corporation name. They had not owned that house as Rory and Cade Lyman. But she could not remember the name. She couldn't even remember the city.

How old had she been when they went to that house? If she had been small enough for a booster seat, the visit had been long before the decision to flee. But if she'd been tall enough and heavy enough for a regular seat belt, perhaps her mother and father had actually been double-checking their getaway location when they took that drive. But Murielle would have paid no attention to the drive. She'd have been slumped in the back with a doll and video, and would have never looked out the window.

Cathy had been studying her Latin on the computer. It was not off, merely sleeping. She touched a key to bring it back and pulled up a map of Connecticut. For such a tiny state, there were a lot of little cities. Bridgeport? Stratford? New London? Groton? East Hartford? Ansonia?

Ansonia sounded familiar.

She Googled a map of Ansonia, a pointless exercise. Murielle of long ago would never have known the street name. Very quickly she learned that there was such a thing as property records, and that Ansonia's were online. In moments, she had passed through the city Web site and into something called Vision Appraisal, which did not require a password. Property records were public. She entered "Lyman" for the property owner's name.

No one named Lyman came up.

She tried first names: Cade. Rory.

No.

She looked at all the video materials that could be pulled up—street views, real estate sales. She learned nothing.

It occurred to her that the word "Ansonia" probably just looked familiar because it had sort of a Latin ending, like a Roman girl's name. I don't actually remember this city, thought Cathy tiredly. I've just been studying a bunch of Latin lately.

She was moving the cursor to close the screen when she realized there was one name she had not looked up. She went back to the property lists and typed "Murielle." There was no "Murielle." But alphabetically, ahead of where "Murielle" would have been was "Mure Corporation."

Daddy and Mommy had called her Mure. Aunt Lois, who thought the name Murielle was heavy-duty and a ridiculous choice for a little girl, had called her Muffin. Strangers called her Muriel. But Daddy and Mommy said Mure.

She followed the material. She could not tell who owned the Mure Corporation. But whoever they were, they had a house at 98 West Valley Road. And Vision Appraisal, not surprisingly, supplied a photograph.

It *was* a triple-decker.

But in her wildest dreams, she could not imagine Rory and Cade living in such a place, not even for a night. A broken aluminum lawn chair leaned against a rusting fire escape. An ancient sedan was parked on the grass. On the tiny second-floor porch, a geranium blossomed in a coffee can, while laundry hung on strings run from one side of the porch to the other. On the tiny third-floor porch, somebody was sitting in the shade. No features could be distinguished.

It's not them, she told herself. If they ever stayed there, it was five years ago, for a minute.

Rory and Cade had millions of dollars. They weren't going to carry dirty clothes to a launderette or tote groceries up two flights or park their junker in the yard. Rory and Cade could not blend in here. Rory would be wearing shoes that cost more than the neighbors paid for a month's rent. Rory wasn't going to shop like her neighbors. No day-old bread. No seconds on sheets. No ancient used car bought for cash. Rory wouldn't set foot in Target, or Sears, or Wal-Mart or Kmart or T.J. Maxx or any store where the people who lived in that triple-decker shopped.

Where *we* shop, thought Cathy ruefully, thinking of her foster family. Where we shop carefully.

Rory and Cade surely led a beautiful life among beautiful people, and that would be their disguise, because they would fit in easily and blend well. Daddy would learn polo. They would summer at a rented chateau in France and winter in a ski resort in Switzerland. They might fish in Scotland and sail the Mediterranean.

It was ludicrous to think they could be—or had been—twenty-five miles away.

The feverish excitement abated. She was just a girl alone in a room with a computer that told her nothing she needed.

What she needed was sleep.

Or a reverse phone directory. She could look up 98 West Valley and get the phone numbers for the three apartments. She could call them. They would not be Rory and Cade. But they might send rent checks to Rory and Cade. At the very least, they would have an address for the Mure Corporation.

The reverse phone check took a while. Every time she thought she was there, it zipped her to a site where she had to pay. She didn't want to pay. She couldn't pay; she didn't have a credit card. Finally she located a free site and up came two phone numbers. Perhaps the third family had only a cell phone.

Perhaps the third family always used prepaid disposable cell phones. Perhaps their real names were Rory and Cade.

Nonsense. She was losing sleep and study time in a pathetic attempt to succeed where the combined intelligence of the IRS, the SEC, the NASD, the FBI and all the other initials people had failed.

Suddenly she could not remember what Rory and Cade looked like.

Panic set in.

She bookmarked her search pages and closed them.

In the olden days, when asked what you would save if your house burned down, you might have answered, "Photo albums." But Murielle's parents had kept their photographs online. She had retrieved the file when she first moved here. She could access the pictures anytime she wanted.

She rarely wanted.

Her favorite photograph had been taken that final Christmas before it all went down. She and Mommy and Daddy were going to Aunt Lois's house for Christmas dinner. All three were dressed in Christmas colors: Daddy in a white shirt with red suspenders and a Santa bow tie; Mommy in a slim red dress and green earrings; Murielle in a green dress embroidered with red trees.

Around little Murielle was a heap of packages, beautifully wrapped and beribboned. She could not remember the contents of a single one.

Her first Christmas as a foster child had been in this house. She and Marmee and Dad Bob (but not Jamesy, who hadn't come for three more years) had gone to a Christmas tree farm. Cathy got to choose the tree, and they put it up together, and it was too wide. Dad Bob took out the coffee table so the tree branches would fit.

Christmas Eve she had wondered whether the tree would have anything under it for her, because Mommy and Daddy did not have her address, nor for that matter her name.

How thrilled she had been to find that she still got to have Christmas. There were two open shopping bags, the pretty department-store kind with twine handles. One was big and one was little. The big one was a Santa Sack from a church: hers had been filled to match a little tag reading *Ten-Year-Old Girl*. It had two books, neither of which she had read: *The Best Christmas Pageant Ever,* which made her weep, and *Black Beauty,* which really made her weep. There was a beautiful sweater, just for the shoulders, called a shrug. It was lacy and pink and dripped with ribbons and sequins. There were bedroom slippers, fat and puffy, a paint set, a diary and two cute little hairbands.

She never told Marmee and Dad Bob that in a home now sold at auction she had had hundreds of these, better-quality and stored in beautiful furniture in beautiful rooms. She could remember her past condition, but it was too different to seem real. Real was her life with Marmee and Dad Bob. Real was one sweater, not dozens.

The second Christmas shopping bag contained only envelopes. Each envelope had a photograph. There were a horse photo, a tennis photo, a piano photo, a flute photo, a gymnastics photo and a dance photo. Marmee said, "Lessons are waiting for you. A friend at church is going to pay for them. You choose one. Which do you want to do each week?"

She had done all but flute in her previous life. She remembered all her lessons so fondly. The stable. The courts. The Bach. The balance beam. The dance shoes.

All that Christmas Day long, she shuffled pictures, and she was still deciding when they left for Christmas dinner at Grammy's. In the end, Murielle picked tennis. Somewhere out there, Mommy and Daddy would be glad that she was working on her tennis.

Cathy Ferris stared at the Christmas photograph and the strangers who were her real parents. "I've been hiding, too," she whispered. "Should I come out? Is it safe to be Murielle?"

They did not answer.

Even now she could not bear to think that they did not care.

Tommy Petrak was beginning to question the concept of cramming two semesters of Chinese into six weeks of class. He could study all night and not make a dent. Of course, he could study better if his nerves weren't jarred; if he didn't keep glancing at the picture on his cell phone and wondering about Cathy Ferris.

It was well into the night when he realized that his parents were still up. This was extraordinary. After they watched the ten o'clock news, they went to bed. Seven days a week. They led boring lives. They had long ago stopped checking on his bedtime, which was good, because rarely did he consider sleep before midnight. You could not be an honor roll student and get eight hours of sleep.

Here it was one in the morning and they were downstairs talking.

No. Arguing.

He hated to hear his parents argue. During the terrible months after Rory and Cade had run, his mother had been trapped on the edge of the investigation, and his father so furious and frightened that Tommy thought they might get a divorce.

He still remembered that bank statement showing the million-dollar deposit.

It was a huge sum to a family like the Petraks. Tommy had admired all the zeros. Had had a long mental list of what they could buy and do.

And now his stupid decision to forward a photograph had ignited the fights again. He walked downstairs. He made no attempt to be quiet, but since the voices in the kitchen were raised, his footsteps went unheard. He was startled to realize that the man talking so angrily in his kitchen at one in the morning was not his father.

"You did the right thing to call me, Travis," said the male voice.

Tommy recognized the voice. *No, he can't be here. Don't let him be here. Don't let this start up again!*

"I cannot believe, Mrs. Petrak," said Matt Keefer, "that you never told us you've had six phone calls from Rory over the years."

Six? Tommy had known about one. We're in trouble, he thought.

He remembered that terrible week when Julianna's mother was arrested. Julianna came to school with her head up, her teeth gritted, her cheeks permanently flushed. Are we next? he thought, frightened.

"I'm willing to let that slide," said the FBI agent, "if we can use the girl."

His mother's voice cracked. "You cannot use that child!"

"You were going to use her five years ago. The reason

you lost Murielle to foster care was not the payoff sitting in your account. It was because the caseworker was horrified at your plan to use little Murielle. You finished yourself off as a guardian for your niece."

Tommy wanted to beat the guy up. He wanted his father to beat the guy up. But first he needed to know what they were talking about.

His mother was shouting. "I was scared. I was furious. I lashed out. I wouldn't have done it. I dropped the idea in the same sentence I presented it. You know that, Matt Keefer! Anyway, this is not Murielle. This is some girl studying Latin."

His mother did not believe this. She believed Cathy was Murielle. She was heartbroken that Cathy had not accepted her. All through dinner she had come up with plans to convince Cathy—Murielle—that her aunt Lois could be trusted after all.

"It probably wouldn't have worked back then anyway, Mrs. Petrak," said the agent. "Rory and Cade would have known it was a ploy. But five years later? I think it's brilliant. And it will work. I want Rory and Cade in prison until they're old and gray. We'll use Cathy Ferris as bait. Rory and Cade will walk right into the trap."

· 12 ·

Murielle

TV had not had a big place at Murielle's house. Her parents were too busy, and when they had free time, the Internet consumed them. Or sports. They were often up at dawn, playing tennis on their private court as soon as there was enough light to see the lime-green tennis balls. They were fond of baseball, too, but listened on the radio, so they could do something else at the same time.

Murielle had started French, swimming, horseback riding, soccer and gymnastics before she entered kindergarten. Then she added dance, piano and tennis. What with school, study, practice, rehearsals and lessons, Murielle hardly ever glanced at a television.

The second foster mother and father liked talk shows as much as the first ones had. Murielle had supper (or, more correctly, supper was served; Murielle had very little of it) as an angry host screamed about corporate criminals damaging the economy and mocking society. Rory and Cade Lyman were examples.

The second family kept kids of all ages—they had a newborn and a toddler when she arrived. It was wonderful to rock the baby and show the toddler how to steer a crayon.

Right away, one of those initials people showed up. She pretended not to recognize Matt Keefer. But in fact she was desperately glad to see him, and praying he would take her back to her house, and maybe he would even know something about her parents.

"Hi, Muriel," he said. "How are you doing?" He handed her a suitcase. "Your aunt Lois packed it," he said. "Now you have enough."

Enough what? What about her stuffed animals and winter clothes and shoes and violin? What about her doll-houses and jewelry and skis? What about her bicycles and tennis rackets? What about her house and her home and her mother and father?

Matt Keefer squatted down beside her and bounced around on his heels.

He asked question after question.

He was clever. Over and over again she felt herself starting to answer.

It seemed easier just to throw up again, and that got rid of him.

In the dining room—where nobody dined; it was more of an office and a storeroom—her second foster home had a computer so old and slow, Murielle felt as if she were personally carrying the Internet connections around the country. Her parents had taken the paper edition of the *Greenwich Time,* which was delivered to the house. Maybe the online newspaper would have an article explaining what was happening! The TV talk shows just talked about money. But she needed other stuff. Maybe a paragraph in the *Greenwich Time* would supply the missing facts. She could gauge when Daddy was coming for her.

Murielle opened the home page of the *Greenwich Time*, and right there was an interview with Aunt Lois: Local Woman Relieved as Ordeal Ends. In smaller print: Grateful to Be Exonerated Says Sister of Missing Criminal.

The article said that the FBI believed Lois Petrak had known that her sister and brother-in-law planned to flee the country, had been helping them and was therefore an accessory. However, they were not going to pursue this case further. But they would seize the Lymans' huge house in Greenwich. House and contents would be sold.

Murielle stared around the small dark rooms of the foster home.

Mrs. O'Neill had said this was just for a few days. But that was a lie. Because there would be no home to go back to.

Murielle had not known that grown-ups lied. She had not known that her parents would lie. She had not known . . . well . . . anything.

Murielle read on. "How do you feel toward your sister?" the reporter asked Lois Petrak.

"I hate her for putting us through this."

"If your sister tried to get in touch, what would you do?"

"I'd turn her in."

Murielle gasped. Not only would Aunt Lois be glad if Mommy got handcuffed. *She'd help.*

Then it was Sunday.

Murielle opened the suitcase packed by her aunt, ignoring the note on top. She stepped into a pretty dress, and chose socks with lace trim and white Mary Janes. When she went into the TV room, the foster mother and father stared at her blankly. Murielle had gone to Sunday school almost every Sunday of her life. She was just as blank. Why weren't they ready? She had to talk this time. "Are we going to church?"

"Church . . . ," said the foster mother as if she didn't use the word often. "Okay. Sure. What kind of church?"

Murielle had not known there were kinds of church. They just went.

"What's the name of your church at home?" asked the foster mother.

Murielle felt panic. She didn't think of it as having a name. It was just church. "It's okay. I don't have to go." She blinked hard against the tears, but a sob was rising inside her, and she could feel that it planned to leap out, and she was going to bawl, big loud heaves, like the calf last year in church when they were giving money to the Heifer Project so that children all over the world would have their own herds, and somebody had brought in a real calf, which bawled for its mother while the children giggled and touched its soft hide.

"I haven't been to church in years," said the foster father. "This is as good a time as any. Let's go."

The foster father drove to a big brick building like an elementary school. When they walked in, she could tell it was a church, but not like her own. She sat in the pew. She felt like a broken pencil. She didn't sing the hymns. When

110

the other children left for Sunday school, she didn't follow. Then the minister said it was time for silent prayer and everybody must pray for what they needed most.

I need my parents. I need my house. I need my friends. I need my stuff. I need my cell phone.

"Now," said the minister, "let us give thanks to the Lord."

Murielle could think of nothing to be thankful for.

The minister gave little tips. "Our homes," he said, leaving a few moments of silence so you could think about your home. "Our loving families. Laughter."

Murielle usually filled in the *o*'s in the church bulletin during sermons, but it was too much effort this morning. She read the bulletin instead. The last page listed the Ten Commandments. Murielle considered them.

I don't worship other gods. I don't have idols. I don't swear. I'm keeping the Sabbath holy. I honor my father and mother.

She got a little off track. Had they honored her? Had they honored their own parents, no longer alive, but still . . .

She read on. She hadn't murdered anybody. She hadn't committed adultery. Actually, she had never even held hands.

Number eight: do not steal.

Number nine: do not lie.

It was beginning to look as if her mother and father had broken eight and nine big-time. Happily. Had fun. High-fived at the rental car counter.

As for number ten, the word "covet" was unknown to her, and she didn't have her cell phone to look it up in a dictionary.

There was a final hymn, and she knew it well. She stayed silent. Singing, like being thankful, was for other people.

On the sixth day of captivity at the second foster home, the foster mother and father sat at the big table, examining a map of the state of Connecticut. It was the folding kind, with cities in blocks and rectangles along the edges.

Connecticut itself was a rectangle, with water—Long Island Sound, a finger of the Atlantic Ocean—along the bottom and Massachusetts across the top. Greenwich was a funny little toe poking off the left toward New York City.

"Where are we?" she asked.

The foster mother put an arm around her and gathered her in. Murielle let it happen. "We're in Stratford. It's pretty far from Greenwich, where you lived." She drew her fingernail along the highway back to where Murielle had grown up. She gave a little map lesson. "This line is I-95, the road you took to get here. This line, with the little crosshatches, is the railroad, which goes through Greenwich and all the way to New York City."

Murielle pointed to the box in which Stratford was enlarged. "Where is this house?"

"Right here."

That night the foster father locked the doors, and the foster mother tucked Murielle into bed and gave her a kiss and said that everything would look better in the morning.

Murielle slept, jerking awake every hour or so. When she woke up around five a.m., it was starting to get light. She crept out of bed, dressed carefully, put a few things into her backpack and tiptoed out of the house. A few miles later she was at the railroad station. Even this early, there were many commuters also taking the train.

Trains were fun for a few minutes and then they were boring. You had to have a book. Luckily Mommy had put two books in the new backpack. Murielle went to the ticket window. She was short but she could see over the top of the counter, and she said politely, "One-way to Greenwich, please."

The ticket man smiled, but seemed puzzled. "Traveling alone?"

"Yes."

"Where are Mom and Dad?"

Murielle had not expected this. She said carefully, "They'll meet me there."

He was not satisfied.

"My aunt and uncle are waiting outside. They're letting me handle the transaction myself." She made herself smile. The man smiled back. "You're doing a great job," he said.

She would take the train to Greenwich and then a taxi to her house. She didn't have a key, but she knew how to get in without one. She had to get inside fast and race to the control panel in time to disable the alarm system.

She handed over a one-hundred-dollar bill. The ticket man's expression changed. What was wrong? She had checked the fare. She'd given him enough.

"This is a lot of money," he said.

What was the problem with that?

"Okay," he said slowly. "You stay right there and I'll be back with the ticket."

But he was not back with the ticket.

He was back with a policeman.

They opened her backpack and found the rest of the money. And pretty soon she was not back at the second foster home. She was in an office, sitting on the edge of a desk so that she was higher up and they could talk to her better, and they said, "Honey, are you trying to get to your mom and dad? Where are they? We're hoping to talk to them."

It was important to get home. She had to make them understand. After dry swallows, she said, "I'm just going home. I don't want a foster family. The housekeeper is there, so I won't be by myself."

"We don't let ten-year-olds live on their own. The housekeeper left because there's nobody to pay her salary. The house is empty. You can't go back."

She couldn't go back? Her own house?

Murielle held Aunt Lois responsible. She would gladly have gone into exile with her parents. Now she was in exile without them.

She wished she could be Latisha and throw a fit and get her way. But she just stood there, defeated.

A youngish man with a funny little beard, like a square of Velcro stuck on his pointy chin, drove her back to the foster home, where the foster mother said, "Cathy, honey, we don't keep runaways. It's too much responsibility. So you're going to another house. You be a good girl for them, okay?"

Murielle got all As. She never skipped piano practice. She learned her French, found time for her violin, tried

114

hard in swimming, cheerfully groomed the ponies at the stable. In her two foster homes, she had helped with dishes and babies. Wasn't that being a good girl?

"Cathy doesn't eat well," the foster mother told the young man. "Try to get her to eat."

In the car, the young man gave her an energy bar. She did not have enough energy to unwrap it. They drove into the glare of the sun, and the young man unwrapped it for her, but it was all bumpy and gross, with grainy bits nobody could identify.

They drove forever. Every drive Murielle ever took with a social worker lasted forever. Finally, they were walking up a strange path, climbing strange steps, entering a strange house, and strange people were taking her little suitcase and her new backpack. It wasn't new anymore. It was raggy.

"I'm Bob Ferris," said the new foster father, kneeling down beside her. "You can call me Uncle Bob, or Dad, or Mr. Ferris, or whatever works for you, Cathy. Our last kid called me Dad Bob." He puffed his lips around the *d*'s and the *b*'s, making Dad Bob sound so silly she almost smiled.

"And I'm Marnie Ferris," said the new foster mother, giving her a hug. "You can call me Mom, or Mrs. Ferris, or Marnie."

"Marmee?" said Murielle, misunderstanding. "Once my mother and I saw a movie called *Little Women*. Meg, Jo, Beth and Amy called their mother Marmee."

"I loved that movie too. Actually there's more than one movie of *Little Women*. And the book is great. Did you and your mother read the book? No? Maybe you and I will read it. I love to read aloud." Marmee took Murielle's hand.

"Meanwhile, how about a sandwich, Cathy? Do you like tuna fish, peanut butter, grilled cheese or plain old toast?"

"Not tuna." Murielle hoped Marmee would do all the reading so she could do all the listening. Maybe she would explain that her name was not really Cathy.

But Marmee said, "I love the name Cathy. Do you spell it with a *C* or a *K*? Cathy *C* and Kathy *K* are completely different names, you know."

A little square of sunlight brightened the kitchen where they stood. She held her hands out for the sun.

"Tell you what," said Marmee. "Let's make one sandwich of each kind, except for tuna, of course—we won't open a can of tuna, no sirree—and we'll cut the sandwiches into quarters and fix a platter and then decide which ones to eat. Do you like your crusts on or off?"

"Off."

"Me too. We'll save the crusts and make meat loaf. Do you like meat loaf? Mostly only grown-ups like meat loaf. I'll fix you something else. You're our only daughter right now, you know. Usually we have two kids, but everybody else went home. Now after we've had our sandwiches and we've read a chapter in *Little Women,* we are going shopping. You are low low low low on clothes."

Dad Bob and Marmee were warm and calm, and their talk was warm and calm. The house was filled with pleasant routines. The only television was old and they got just basic cable, which meant that there was little to watch, so instead they rode bikes and went to the park and played board games and cooked supper and listened to music on the radio. Both her Ferris parents worked at the hospital. There were always hospital stories to tell, and some were

116

very sad. "Don't you get sad too?" she asked Dad Bob one day.

"No. Because every day, we know we've done something good in the world. Maybe only for a minute. Still, we made life easier for people who are scared or in pain."

They were certainly making life easier for Murielle Lyman. But they could not produce her parents, even for a minute. Only Mommy and Daddy could make that happen.

But they never came back.

· 13 ·

Cathy

Tommy and his mother were sitting at the breakfast bar. She was tracing patterns in the new granite countertop, ignoring the bacon, eggs and bagel on her plate. His mother loved to eat and did too much of it, too often. He could not remember seeing her fail to eat. She had opened a file on the kitchen computer labeled *Rory Fam Fotos* and was staring at pictures of their last Christmas together, before anybody knew that her sister and brother-in-law were criminals.

Tommy had gotten no answers last night. The agent left, his father stalked away, his mother wept, Tommy gave up and went to bed. But something was going to happen, and he was the proximate cause, and he felt defenseless. He needed weapons, or at least knowledge. He moved carefully because his mother could sink into despair and silence when the topic was Murielle or fly into seething fury when the topic was her sister Rory.

He gazed at the Christmas photos. "How come we

always had the holiday dinners? Rory and Cade had the fabulous house."

"They didn't cook. And they meant to decorate for Christmas each year, but they never got around to it. The year before this picture, they hired a decorator to do their tree. It had a theme. I forget what it was. Doves maybe. Another year your father and I bought their tree. We set it up and you and Muffin decorated it."

"Was Muffin sad about that kind of thing?"

"No. It was the way things were. Her parents were glamorous exciting people who popped in every now and then. She adored them." His mother sighed. "I adored them. Their lives were so exciting."

Tommy had been crazy about his aunt Rory and his uncle Cade. They'd been much more fun than his stodgy parents. Rory and Cade certainly never cared whether a person had a balanced life or a balanced diet. But it sounded a little tricky to agree that they had been totally cool, so he said, "Mom, did Aunt Rory really call you six times?"

"Yes."

"What did you talk about?"

His mother shrugged. "We're sisters. We love each other and we hate each other. I always envied her life and she never envied mine."

"When you didn't drive Muffin to the plane, what did Aunt Rory say then?"

"That first call was from Cade. He was mad, but not worried. I was too upset to think of it at the time, but they probably had a plan for returning safely and anonymously to America. I suppose Cade pictured himself strolling in

119

here to collect Muffin. But American television news is available in Europe, or wherever they went—they didn't say and I didn't ask—so they turned on the news in their foreign hotel room and saw our house under siege. Rory called to check on Murielle, but she'd already been taken into foster care. Which I couldn't bring myself to admit. Anyway, I thought it would just be for a night. And Rory figured that media and police attention would slack off and I'd stop being uncooperative and then they'd get Murielle."

"We have caller ID," Tommy pointed out. "So you had a record of the phone number she called from. The FBI could have located her."

"No. She used prepaid cell phones that she used only once. When I tried to call her back, nothing happened. I did write the numbers down. I gave Matt Keefer the list last night. The FBI will try to find out where those particular phones were sold. You know—Paris or Miami."

His mother clicked on through *Rory Fam Fotos* and found a picture of Murielle standing alone in a welter of crumpled wrapping paper. "She's a sad little waif, isn't she? And yet she had her parents' personality. They had huge auditorium-sized personalities. I guess to coax millions of dollars out of people, you have to have a vivid presence. Murielle was popular. Kids loved to be around her, the way clients loved being around Rory."

"How come Murielle never just phoned us, Mom?"

"I'm sure she held me responsible for her separation from her parents. She wouldn't have held Rory and Cade responsible. And if Cathy Ferris is Murielle, she still holds me responsible. She's still mad."

Cathy Ferris had not seemed mad to Tommy. She had seemed detached. He began eating his mother's bagel. "Keep going. The next Rory phone call?" He added more cream cheese.

"I had to admit to her that the Department of Children and Families had taken Murielle. Rory was beside herself, but we agreed that the system would return Murielle any minute. You don't stick a child in foster care unless there's no family at all, or the circumstances are dangerous for the child. But your father and I were under investigation because of that million dollars. Every time Rory called, I just screamed at her. I couldn't talk rationally. I screamed when the authorities were here too, because I was scared and furious. Even now I can't repeat my suggestion for how they could get Rory and Cade to come home. But because of it, they decided I wasn't a fit guardian. Me. Lois Petrak. For my own niece."

Tommy was tired of feeling sorry for his mother. "When was the last call from Aunt Rory?" he demanded.

"Two years ago."

Two years? He was horrified. If they had never heard from Muffin's mother, it would be one thing. But they had heard from her, and then she lost interest? Let two years go by? "What did she say in that last call?"

"Same thing she said in every call. Did we have news about Murielle."

"And did we?"

"No." His mother was crying.

His mother put some egg on her fork. He would feel better if she gave the food her usual serious attention. But she let the egg fall off the fork.

"You know what the worst thing is?" he told his mother. "I accused Cathy of being Murielle right in front of Julianna Benner."

His mother winced. "Whenever I think of the Benners, I am absolutely sick. My sister was a news junkie. She would have been following every bit of coverage on the Internet and on TV. She let Nancy Benner go to prison and she knew it."

"Nancy Benner admitted she knew what was going on."

"But she wasn't the one doing it," said his mother. "If they'd had Rory around to send to prison, they'd have let Nancy Benner off with a fine." She stared at the photograph of little Murielle alone in a Christmas picture. "Tommy, when that girl Cathy walked out of the high school, I saw Rory walking. When she looked at me, I saw Rory's eyes. But when she spoke, I admit I didn't hear Rory's voice. Rory was fierce. When she was little, we called her Tiger. I always felt like prey around her."

Tommy laughed.

His mother didn't. "People were prey to her, you know. Not clients."

He shivered. "Mom, tell me exactly what Matt Keefer's going to do. I'll be in school with Cathy in half an hour. In what way does he plan to use her?"

Cathy had not begun to study until two a.m. It took that long to deal with the hardness in her heart. She managed a few hours' sleep and crawled out of bed. Her mind was spinning with Latin to the point that English was difficult. She packed a lunch because she needed to look like

122

everybody else in the student center, not because she imagined herself eating it.

Marmee got Jamesy ready for day care. Dad Bob was long gone, because his shift began so early.

Cathy poured Cheerios into a bowl and pretended to add milk and pretended to eat standing up, looking out the kitchen window at the weather. When Marmee wasn't looking, Cathy slid the dry Cheerios back into the box. She couldn't manage food and emotion at the same time.

The phone rang.

Marmee glanced at the caller ID and flinched. She pressed her lips together, looking almost frightened. "Marmee?" said Cathy, alarmed.

Marmee snapped at her. "Put Jamesy in his car seat for me. And eat something!"

Cathy was resentful. She hadn't done anything to deserve getting yelled at. Well—except to fake eating and skip studying and lie about summer school and not mention that Murielle Lyman was back in the picture.

Jamesy didn't want to go to school. She had to drag him out the door, while Marmee stood there with her arms folded, letting the phone ring. Out on the grass, Jamesy refused to walk. "Please be a big helper," said Cathy. "We don't have much time. I don't want to be late for my car pool."

Jamesy didn't want to be a big helper.

"How about being a little helper?" she said. "Could you be a miniature two-second helper?"

Jamesy giggled. "Then I'm already done helping." But he climbed into his car seat and let her deal with the straps.

She worried momentarily about the phone call. It was probably nothing. In the morning, they were always frantic. It was probably somebody who talked a lot, and Marmee didn't have time. Cathy ran back in for her book bag and lunch. Marmee was on the phone. "I have to run," she said in a strained voice. "I can't talk now." She hung up, looked vaguely around the kitchen, found her handbag and zipped it in a clumsy nervous way.

Money? thought Cathy. Unpaid bills? Are we in trouble?

She felt better. Money trouble was lousy, but it was normal. Normal for the Ferris family, anyway. She had the sudden thought that Murielle Lyman was probably wealthy.

Even last week, Cathy would have wanted the money. How much easier Marmee and Dad's lives would be. A new car, a new kitchen, a new washer and dryer. A good vacation, more meals out. But now she knew about Julianna.

Oh, Mommy! Oh, Daddy! If I ever find you, what will I think of you?

There was no anger. No boiling rage. Just a profound sadness.

In the car, Marmee put on the radio for the weather while Jamesy said over and over that he didn't want to go to school, and Marmee said, "Please, please, please, Jamesy." She sounded close to tears.

"Marmee?"said Cathy again.

"Later," said Marmee, presumably meaning "I'll tell you later." "Here we are." She pulled into the commuter lot, where Mrs. Tartaglia was waiting.

"I'm sorry," Marmee shouted through her open window. "I didn't think we were late!"

"You're not late! I'm early! Hi, Cathy!" Mrs. Tartaglia was smiling. She looked very elegant. Spencer was grinning at her. He was sitting in the backseat this time, so they could talk more easily. Cathy jumped out of her car, said "Bye!" over her shoulder and hopped into the Tartaglias' Lexus.

Mrs. Tartaglia was out of the parking lot as if on the Indy Speedway.

"We're not late," Spencer explained, "but Mom has a chance to go into the city with her girlfriends, and they're catching the train in Stamford and she's catching it in Greenwich after she drops us off, and she's going to have trouble getting a parking space, so we're speeding to give her that crucial extra sixty seconds."

"Cool." It was nice having Spencer sitting back here. She felt less like a chore and more like a friend. She felt one hundred percent Cathy. It was a clean smooth feeling, as if the wrinkles of Murielle had been ironed away. "What will you do in the city, Mrs. Tartaglia?"

"There's an exhibit at the Metropolitan Museum," said Mrs. Tartaglia.

"Which is true," said Spencer, "but they aren't going to see it. They're going shopping."

"We might see it, though," said Mrs. Tartaglia. "We're pretending we'll go see it." She giggled. "So you and Spencer have to hang out at school longer than usual. Spencer's dad will come for you at four."

Cathy nodded. "We can always use more study time."

"More study time? You kids are remarkable. When I

was your age—oh, well, let's not think about how shallow I was. Still am." Mrs. Tartaglia sang at the top of her lungs, "Start spreading the news. . . . I'm leaving today. . . . I want to be a part of it—New York, New York."

Spencer added the rhythm: "Dum, dum, dahhhh-dah dum!"

Then they sang "Take Me Out to the Ball Game," which, strictly speaking, was not a New York song, but Spencer had only ever sung it at Yankee Stadium.

Miraculously they hit no serious traffic and Mrs. Tartaglia dropped them at school. Spencer and Cathy shouted, "Have a good time!" and Mrs. Tartaglia said, "There's no other kind in New York!"

On the sidewalk, Cathy soaked up nice ordinary sun. How satisfyingly schoolish everything looked: all those bricks, all these kids.

"Did you have time for Latin last night?" asked Spencer.

"I did Latin all night. I'm a Latin zombie. How was Arabic?"

"I mainly Googled the Lymans."

Cathy turned into Murielle Lyman, feeling as naked as the day she was born, and as helpless. She took her hair out of the scrunchie, ran her fingers through it, put her hair back in a ponytail and shook it out. I'd better eat something, she thought. She opened a pack of peanut butter crackers and nibbled. It was a good choice. Her nerves began to settle. She started on a second cracker.

"Everybody but you is riveted," said Spencer. "Ava and Meg and Graydon and I were IM'ing all night while you were joyfully memorizing verbs."

Cathy was not going there. She stayed with her dead language. "Want me to display some knowledge?"

"No. I don't want to be confused. I'm shaky in Arabic. Of course, it would help if I had studied Arabic instead of the Lymans."

Cars entered the student parking lot and their drivers walked over to the entrance. Other cars entered the drop-off lane, parents calling good-bye as their son or daughter got out, and then driving away. Meg appeared, and Ava, and Ethan. Colton had ridden his bike, and Julianna materialized out of nowhere.

Two cars turned into visitor parking spaces. Tommy Petrak got out of one. Why hadn't he parked in the student lot?

Tommy looked up, saw Cathy and froze.

An older man got out of the other vehicle. Tommy and the man were not together, but they looked at each other and seemed to synchronize movements, and when Tommy glanced across the courtyard in her direction and then back at the older man, Cathy knew that a signal had been given.

Cathy choked on the second cracker.

"Want some water?" asked Spencer, taking a fresh bottle out of his backpack and opening it for her.

She could not take her eyes off Thomas. Near him, the older man adjusted the lapels of his jacket, tugged lightly on his tie and stepped forward into the sun.

She knew now how Tommy had recognized her. Important people register in your brain. You store their images forever. It does not matter that you have not thought about the other person except in nightmares. It does not

127

matter if you were with that other person only an hour here and ten minutes there.

He had less hair, and what remained was gray. His suit was charcoal, not navy blue. And she knew him.

Matt Keefer was not here to ask how Latin was going.

He was here to find Rory and Cade.

· 14 ·

Murielle

Whenever she said Dad Bob, she got the consonants mixed up. She was just as likely to call him Bad Dob. Slowly, she began saying Dad.

Her own new name, Cathy, was gentle and floating. It didn't seem to have any problems, and when she heard the word "Cathy," she didn't have Murielle to drag around. She felt safe inside the name Cathy, like somebody else. It seemed to her that if she became Cathy Ferris, she really would be somebody else. And she would get to stay with Marmee and Dad, and not change foster homes every few weeks. She would be theirs.

Fifth grade began the last week in August on a hot sweaty too-bright day. Murielle didn't want to go. She couldn't breathe in the sticky air. She walked close to Marmee. She had a new notebook, new pencils and a lot of anxiety. She hadn't eaten much for two days. She walked slower and slower, until they came to a stop. Mrs.

Ferris sat down on the grass. She patted the grass beside her. "Tell me, honey."

"They'll have my name on the attendance list. Murielle Lyman."

"Yes. But I met with your teacher yesterday and she's going to call you Cathy. I promise."

"Could I use your name instead? Could I be Cathy Ferris?"

"Honey, I don't think anybody at this school has heard of your mommy and daddy. But even if they do know sad things about them, they are not going to realize that you're related."

That aspect had not occurred to Murielle. She saw the new name merely as a way to bind herself to the third foster home. "I promise to eat lunch and never skip a meal," said Murielle, making her most generous offer.

Mrs. Ferris got to her feet. "Then let's ask the principal. I'm not sure whether he'll agree or how they'll manage that in the computer system. But I can tell him about your promise to have lunch and maybe he'll say yes."

He said yes.

Of course, nobody expected her to stay very long. Foster children aren't permanent. The principal was being kind and the change was temporary.

Except it wasn't.

Murielle developed a hobby of following the fates of people who ran big companies or invested big sums and got caught doing something criminal. The illegal activities were always about money. People loved money. Murielle had always been surrounded by so much of it that she never thought about it. But it turned out that everybody wanted to be surrounded by money. Some people were honest and worked for it. Others saw a chance to snatch extra money.

People who did this believed that nobody would ever find out: they were too smart; they had stolen too cleverly. And once they were discovered, they also never expected punishment: they were too good for that; they led lives that didn't include hurty scary things. And so they were brought down in horrible public trials that ended in weeping spouses and stunned children and long prison sentences.

But Rory and Cade Lyman had left no trace.

By the time Cathy Ferris was fifteen, and on tennis team and field hockey, an outstanding student, wishing she had more money for clothes and concerned over which shampoo to use and what college to consider, she had stopped looking things up. High school kids talked of the future. Try out for this, rehearse for that. Study this, major in that. Practice this, get a job in that.

The past receded, becoming a thin line on a horizon she no longer looked at.

She had managed to gather good memories of her parents, which she kept like a mental diary.

How every Fourth of July, they went to their house in the Hamptons. They played the same beach volleyball, swam the same laps and always found a few pieces of beach glass to take home. Baked the same flag cake, with strawberries and blueberries in whipped-cream icing. She could see her father's hand, carefully positioning the rows of strawberries to stripe the flag. She could see her mother bending over her, tucking a stray curl back, lightly planting a kiss on her forehead. She could hear the discussion over whether to take the ice cream out of the freezer early to soften it (Mom) or leave it rock hard (Dad). Whether to scoop it out (Mom) or open the paper packaging and cut it in slices (Dad). In her memory, neither parent dropped everything to check messages, make calls or study printouts.

Every now and then she'd run an online search for Rory and Cade in the *Wall Street Journal,* the likeliest source for news about missing financiers. As for the *Greenwich Time,* it was years since that Web site had mentioned their celebrity-status fugitive couple.

But a few months ago, seated in front of her computer, writing a history paper, Cathy Ferris glanced at the date and realized that the fifth anniversary of her parents' flight was coming up.

She had closed the file she'd been working on and gone to the Internet. She pulled up the front page of the *Greenwich Time* to see if there was a retrospective article. Instead, she found a story about Greenwich High's unusual summer school. Listed among local students who planned to participate was Thomas Petrak, who had a lifelong interest in China and planned to study Chinese.

Tommy. Her beloved cousin Tommy. Who had yelled at her in such fear and fury that terrible night. Her heart had leaped with longing to see him.

How amazing that he had had a lifelong interest in China.

Did she, Cathy, have lifelong interests? Other than wondering about Rory and Cade? Hope blew through her brain. *If her parents had tried to find her, Tommy would know.*

She clicked to the information page for the summer school. Six hours of a single subject every day! Three hours of weekday homework; many hours of weekend study. It would be a staggering amount of work. It would consume every waking minute of every day of her summer vacation.

She would do it. At this summer school, she could meet Tommy again. She could find out about Rory and Cade as a stranger, and yet stay a stranger, and be safe inside Cathy Ferris.

She didn't consider Chinese or Arabic for a moment. She didn't have that kind of intelligence. The choice between German and Latin was easy too, because Norwalk High offered Latin and so taking a first-year course actually did make sense; she could add second-year Latin to next year's schedule, which would look great on college applications. Whereas German would be a stranded semester, taking her nowhere.

Marmee and Dad were thrilled by such an impressive goal—studying the classics! They regarded her with awe. The next day, at the guidance office, the counselor was just as excited. "Let's check your grades and scores. They're not going to let just anybody into that program. You'll have to be stellar academically."

She was stellar. She didn't need to check her grades and scores, but nevertheless, she positioned herself to see the counselor's screen. He did not prevent this, although usually school officials were protective of what they regarded as their information. The page said: "Ferris, Cathy." Beneath it, under "Special Information," where you might enter "Diabetic" or "ADHD," it said, "See also Lyman, Catherine."

The name Murielle was not there at all. She felt slightly sick. She took a risk. She said, "What do they have under 'Lyman'?"

"Don't know." He clicked. The screen read, "Lyman, Catherine. See Ferris, Cathy."

The guidance counselor said in his friendly understanding voice, "It's common in divorces, Cathy. Some kids keep their father's last name, but if the mother goes back to her maiden name, sometimes the kids do too. And if there's a stepfather who adopts them, they take his name. And so on. You'd be surprised how many kids are in your situation."

He had no idea she was a foster child. Whatever information had come with her into fifth grade had not moved with her through middle school and into high school. He thought she was a child of divorce.

Nobody named Murielle had ever been in school here. It was terrifying, as if she had died out, like a plant or a tribe.

"Your grades are excellent, Cathy. We've got a good chance of getting you into this language program. You're taking Spanish, I see. You feel comfortable adding a second foreign language?"

"Yes."

He clicked on a download and opened the application for summer school in the town where Murielle Lyman had been born. He entered "Ferris, Cathy."

For the first time, it dawned on her that she herself had prevented her parents from finding her: just as they had ceased to be Rory and Cade Lyman, she had ceased to be Murielle.

We were partners after all, she thought.

The only hard thing to set up was the ride to and from Greenwich. Mrs. Tartaglia was nice about it, but the moment you agree to carpool, your freedom is shot. And Spencer, although he fretted about whether he could do this, was exceedingly smart. It was one of the problems of the whole enterprise: she was among kids who genuinely believed they could learn a year of Arabic in six weeks.

Now, sitting in the courtyard, watching the FBI advance, she wondered if those same kids were smart enough to figure out who she was.

They probably were. But they didn't matter now.

She remembered her parents shredding papers all through that last week. Remembered the computers, and the hard drives, and the FBI setting up an office in her very own house.

My house, thought Cathy. She nearly came up off the bench screaming. *My house!*

At the place she now called home—Bob and Marnie Ferris's house—in her bedroom, sat a computer that was not even turned off. It was asleep. Bookmarked were pages that led to a three-family house in Ansonia. A house that might have been, and might still be, owned by Rory and Cade Lyman. An Internet connection that might take the FBI to the very doorstep where her parents hid. Their true location might possibly be only a few clicks farther into the information pool of the Web.

It would take the FBI ten minutes to discover that there was no such person as Cathy Ferris.

Matt Keefer would go to the Greenwich High headmaster. The headmaster would open Cathy's file. Matt

Keefer would talk to Bob and Marnie Ferris, and her foster parents would agree that Cathy was the daughter of Rory and Cade Lyman. Neither Murielle nor Cathy would be of interest to the FBI. They would want to learn one thing only: was this girl in touch with Rory and Cade? When she said no, why would Matt Keefer believe her? He would insist on looking at her computer because he would assume that whatever her history with Rory and Cade, it would be there. And he would be correct. By lunchtime today, he would have found the bookmarks.

Cathy would be the instrument of her parents' arrest.

After all these years, and all this silence, and all this hiding, she would not be her parents' partner. She would be their betrayer.

· 15 ·

The Double

She took refuge as she had before, hiding in a dead language, pretending to check vocabulary in her Latin text. She could not even recognize the letters. She closed her eyes, tightened her lids and squeezed to bring her sight back. Now she could make out the letters. But she had lost the Latin. In fact, she had lost English. She was wordless with fear.

Her fingers touched the hard grainy surface of the poured concrete and she was assaulted by memory. Wet pajamas, twigs in her hair, dirt on her knees, cold concrete against her cheek.

Spencer seemed to have noticed nothing. "Hey, Tommy," he said cheerfully, preparing to jump into the topic of the Lymans. He took no notice of some man walking near Tommy. Adults had their world; teenagers had theirs.

A normal person, Cathy reminded herself, would look up now. Greet the boy who had created yesterday's drama.

Smile in a friendly accepting way. Giggle because she was that fascinating oddity, the double.

So Cathy looked up. "Hi, Tommy," she said. Her voice sounded high and fake. She remembered playing video games with him, and how he always won, and how he loved winning. She dropped her eyes back to her Latin. The letters swarmed up and around the page.

She had to think of other things. Cathy Ferris things. She thought of that phone call early this morning. Had Marmee been afraid or annoyed?

Matt Keefer cleared his throat.

Cathy brought all her abilities to bear on the page in her Latin book. She read silently, "The relative pronoun *qui, quae, quod,* as common in Latin as its English equivalent 'who/which/that,' ordinarily introduces a subordinate clause." It could have been organic chemistry for all it meant to her weakened brain.

Spencer said politely, "Help you, sir?"

Spencer was one of the good guys.

"I'm here to speak to Miss Ferris, if I may."

She even recognized Matt Keefer's voice. She had not known there was such a thing as voice memory. Would she recognize Mommy's voice if she heard it? Daddy's voice?

She fought tears. This would be the worst possible time to break down.

One good thing: the FBI agent had called her Miss Ferris. He didn't yet know that Cathy Ferris did not exist. And so as Cathy Ferris she quelled her tears, lifted her eyebrows questioningly, closed her Wheelock and got to her feet.

"My name is Matt Keefer," he said in a low voice. "May I speak to you for a minute?"

Give him nothing, she thought. Stay courteous. Have witnesses. "Sure," she said.

He gestured to suggest they should withdraw from the press of students, and immediately she knew how to buy time and space. She didn't move. She kept a bright friendly look on her face and waited him out.

Matt Keefer could probably wait anybody out. It was probably part of his job description. But Tommy was too tense for waiting. "He's a special agent with the FBI," said Tommy unhappily.

Cathy repeated loudly, "The FBI?"

Kids who had grown up on TV cop shows, forensic shows, law-partner shows, pathologist shows, beach-cop shows and animal-cop shows heard the letters *FBI* as if over a loudspeaker. The summer school converged.

"The FBI?" said Ethan.

"The FBI!" shrieked Ava. "Totally cool. Can we see your identification? Why are you here? Do you believe Cathy really is Murielle?"

Colton said, "How did you get into the FBI, Mr. Keefer? What track did you take in high school and college?"

"But first," said Spencer, "how did you find out Cathy even exists?"

"It's my fault," said Tommy, who looked ill and peaked. (*Peak*-ed, Marmee pronounced it. For months, she had said of Jamesy, "He still looks *peak*-ed.") Tommy faced Cathy squarely. She remembered decorating a Christmas tree with him. How he let her have all the lower branches. "I'm sorry, Cathy," he said. "But my dad thought that just in case you are Murielle, he should notify the FBI."

I was right, she thought. Aunt Lois and Uncle Travis *are* the enemy.

What was she to do about her computer?

. She had never known about the fate of her parents' computers, either in their offices or at home. Had they taken out the hard drives? When they distributed those black plastic garbage bags of paper evidence, had they also thrown away the virtual evidence? How? Where? When?

And even if there is time tonight, she thought, even if I buy all kinds of time right now, what do I say to Marmee and Dad? Hi, would you give me a ride to the town dump, because the computer you spent so much money on has information that is possibly dangerous to my real parents and I'm going to bury it somewhere?

"You're after a ten-year-old?" Ava asked Matt Keefer. Then she turned to Cathy. "Do you know for sure that you're Cathy Ferris? Do you have memories prior to age ten?"

Everybody except Julianna laughed. She was not backing away this time. She was moving forward.

Had Matt Keefer been involved in Nancy Benner's arrest? Probably. It would have been an extension of the same case. While Cathy looked at the man who had questioned little Murielle—"We're all friends here! We're all a little worried about Mom and Dad!"—was Julianna looking at the man who said, "You're under arrest, Mrs. Benner"?

Cathy's stomach knotted. She refused to be the conduit that would allow Matt Keefer to say, "You're under arrest,

140

Mrs. Lyman." "Do you have a business card?" she asked politely.

He handed her his card. Ava crowded close to see, so Cathy let Ava take the card, and Ava passed it on. When it got to Julianna, she kept it.

"My dad thought you'd come," Meg told the FBI agent. "He says the statute of limitations applies to the Lymans, and pretty soon the six years will be up, and nobody can bring charges against them, and they can just waltz home and laugh at the people they ripped off."

Her parents could just come home?

Hope lifted every muscle and fiber of her being. She imagined them with a big paper calendar on which they crossed off the weeks.

She imagined seeing them in the distance as they came into focus, and she imagined how wide their smiles were, how their arms were lifted up to hug her, how they started to run toward her.

At what point, Ava had asked yesterday, would a mother and a father decide that money and freedom mattered more than their child? Cathy did not know the answer to that question. But at what point does the child stop hoping that Mommy and Daddy will come?

The answer to that was easy.

Never. A child never stops hoping.

She was buoyant, giddy, with hope. *They can just come home.*

Julianna's features turned grim. Rory and Cade could just come home?

"No," said Mr. Keefer gently. "The statute of limitations might apply if the Lymans had stayed in Greenwich. Then

141

it would be our fault for not charging them in a timely fashion, because there is a five- or six-year time limit, depending on whether we charged them in New York or Connecticut. But when they fled the country, they made it impossible for us to question them, let alone have them arraigned, so the time frame is disrupted. The statute of limitations does not apply. The Lymans will be indicted the moment we find them."

Arraign. Indict.

For a while, Murielle Lyman had continued to search for references to her parents. She looked up words like "unscrupulous" and tried to fathom how that could have anything to do with Mommy and Daddy. She tried to locate the words used on TV talk shows in her computer dictionary, but failed. Years later, she figured out that "a-rain" had a *g* in it. "In-dite" was "indict," with a *c* in it.

Now Matt Keefer smiled at her. She remembered that smile; remembered sitting on a high shelf or table of some sort that day she tried to buy a train ticket; remembered how they waited for him to come; how he smiled at her. It was a real smile; a kind smile. She realized now that he had always pitied her—the fate of being Rory and Cade's daughter. "Miss Ferris, may I speak to you privately?" he asked. "Just for a minute, before class starts."

He would want to talk in a remote adult place, like the principal's office. Greenwich did not refer to people who ran schools as principals. Greenwich had headmasters. Spencer thought it was a riot.

"Nooooo!" wailed Ava. "Don't talk to him privately, Cathy! We don't want to miss anything."

I'm her entertainment, thought Cathy. A nice break

from academics. The possible double, and the arrest and indictment of her parents.

"It's eight-forty-five," said Graydon in a sharp carrying voice. "Class is starting."

These were overachievers and then some. They did not want to miss a minute of class. They had all studied for hours last night and were eager to prove it or ask questions about it. On the other hand, they didn't want to miss anything involving celebrity-status fugitives and the FBI.

"How about lunch hour?" suggested somebody. "We'll all be around at lunch."

"This doesn't actually involve all of you, though," explained Mr. Keefer. He was laughing. He was comfortable with them. She had an image of him coaching his own children's sports.

"Cathy, remember that you can call the shots," said Ava. "Negotiate. Explain that this does involve all of us."

Rory must have been like Ava. Way too pushy, but lots of fun.

The headmaster appeared. "People," Dr. Bella said prissily, "let's get to class."

"But the FBI is here," said Meg.

Cathy saw immediately that the FBI was in trouble. The headmaster controlled this building, not the special agent who trespassed without his permission.

The Latin students went upstairs together.

For three hours, she really was two people.

Cathy Ferris was a smart person who could remember her Latin homework, translate, conjugate, decline and read aloud.

Murielle was not nearly that smart. Murielle could not come up with a single solution to the existence of the computer bookmarks and the easily retrieved history of her online research. Nor to the problem of Matt Keefer, who, if he didn't talk to her today, would just come another day. Nor to the problem of Aunt Lois or Tommy or Ansonia or a statute of limitations that did not apply.

My parents can't ever come home, thought Murielle. She wanted to break things, like Jamesy, or have a tantrum, like Latisha all those years ago.

"The active infinitives for the verb 'to do' or 'to act,'" said Mrs. Shaw.

"*Agere*, 'to do,'" said Cathy. "*Egisse*, 'to have done.' *Acturus*, 'to be going to do.'"

Unless my parents are as brave as Mrs. Benner, thought Murielle. Well, probably Mrs. Benner wasn't brave. She was trapped. But if my parents were brave—

If her parents had been brave, they would have stayed to face things five years ago. They were not brave.

"And for the verb *laudo*?" asked Mrs. Shaw.

"*Laudare, laudavisse, laudaturus,*" said Cathy.

If they get caught, how many years would my parents be in prison? wondered Murielle. Two, like Mrs. Benner? No, because they were the masterminds. And because they ran. Because the economy is in worse shape than when they fled, and the court will hold them partly responsible. And maybe, thought Murielle, maybe they are.

Maybe they damaged the Benners and the investors and even America.

She was in danger of getting caught halfway between Murielle and Cathy; of being some other person entirely.

144

She tried to cling to herself. It would be easier if she knew which self she wanted.

"Excuse me, Mrs. Shaw," said an interfering voice. Not the voice of Matt Keefer. Dr. Bella, the headmaster, stepped into the classroom.

The Latin teacher looked up, surprised and immediately worried.

"Cathy Ferris?" asked the headmaster, looking around, not sure who she was.

Cathy wasn't sure either.

Headmasters did not run errands. Headmasters did not fetch students. They had little minions to run their errands. The class was deeply interested.

"I've given Special Agent Keefer permission to talk with you in my office," said Dr. Bella, trying to sound casual.

"Huh?" said Mrs. Shaw, proving that studying the root language of English did not increase vocabulary.

Cathy wanted to snap at the headmaster. The decision of whether or not to talk to Mr. Keefer, she would say fiercely, is mine. And I choose not to.

But she needed less attention, not more. How would a normal fifteen-year-old girl rescue herself? she thought. Parents.

She had to get this right. She needed to sound uncertain. Embarrassed, but willing, and yet uneasy. . . . "Oh, gosh," she began, trying to sound very young. "This is all a little weird. I think my mother and father wouldn't like this." Very true. Rory and Cade would be crazed. "Maybe I'd better not get involved until I ask Mom and Dad," she said.

The headmaster was nodding. It was the safer option.

Let the parents deal with this, not the school. He was relieved.

She didn't look around. She didn't want to know what Julianna was thinking. She didn't want Ava's sharp eyes and sharper mind peering at her. She wanted Mrs. Shaw to continue with the Latin lesson.

But that was not going to happen. It was lunchtime.

Cathy had to walk downstairs to the student center, and by the time she got there, all her classmates would have texted all their friends in the other classes, and all those kids would have texted everybody else: The FBI wants to question Cathy Ferris.

· 16 ·

Cathy

The mascot of Greenwich High was a cardinal. The bright red bird fluttered on a banner and eyed her brightly from signs over the serving windows. The Cardinal Café, however, was closed for the summer. There were vending machines for water, fruit and ice cream, but nothing fattening or fun, like chocolate bars or Fritos.

Her class went down the heavy open stairs in a group, not talking, because their thumbs were too busy texting, and not looking around, because their eyes were on their tiny screens. Only Cathy looked down.

Spencer was standing at the bottom, although his class met on the lower level and didn't use the stairs. He was waiting for her.

Not ten steps behind Spencer stood Tommy Petrak, and not ten steps from him was Special Agent Keefer. Filling the opening of the far door was the headmaster. They were a train, rushing down the tracks to crush her.

Cathy managed a smile for Spencer and he gave her a

big grin. It was so reassuring. She had an ally, a friend, a ride out of here. She beamed at him.

Tommy's jaw fell.

Matt Keefer raised his eyebrows.

She had forgotten that she had Rory's smile.

Spencer probably didn't even know that Tommy and Agent Keefer and the headmaster were behind him. "Hi, Cathy. Is it true, what Graydon texted? The FBI is actually after you?" He was laughing. This was crazy! This was a comic strip! This was such fun!

Everybody laughed. And everybody drew close.

She must not let Matt Keefer see that she was dissolving. She chose a lemon-drop-yellow chair while Spencer took a cardinal-red one next to her. Kids noticed that Spencer from Arabic had decided to sit at the Latin table, but nobody put a boyfriend interpretation on it. Everyone wanted to sit close to Cathy right now and be part of the action. Spencer was her ride, which gave him priority.

Agent Keefer waded through teenagers to get to Cathy.

But these were not teenagers who got out of people's way. These were teenagers who blocked people's way, because they had questions and needed information. They were a seriously well-prepared crowd. The constant texting from kid to kid, friend to friend, Greenwich natives to strangers in town, had identified Matt Keefer to the entire summer school.

In her quest for normalcy, Cathy gave Tommy a cheery little-girl smile and patted the empty navy blue seat next to her. He zoomed right over, as if they were playing musical chairs, and he wasn't sure that place would be available two beats from now.

A boy Cathy did not know—definitely the type who interrupted teachers and derailed speakers—got in Matt Keefer's face. "Where do you think Rory and Cade are, exactly?" he said, loudly enough for everybody to hear, converge and quiet down for the answer.

Matt Keefer did not seem to mind the interruption. He just nodded. "We think they went to a country that does not extradite criminals to the USA."

This implied that the FBI was not looking for Rory and Cade in America. Or specifically, in Ansonia. Cathy *had* to destroy that computer evidence before the FBI got to her house. She must not let them think for one minute that Rory and Cade could be just around the block.

"What countries are those?" asked the kid.

"Namibia. Tunisia. Mongolia. Chad."

"No," said Ava firmly. "The Lymans are not the kind of people who would live in Mongolia or Chad. I can tell by their Greenwich address that they had a fabulous house with an indoor swimming pool, a huge garage with a nice selection of cars and their own tennis courts. They're not living without plumbing."

Matt Keefer was laughing. Did he agree with Ava's thinking? Or was Ava miles away from the truth and that was the funny part?

"*I* think they're dead," said Ethan.

Cathy's heart slammed against her chest.

"Problem with that is, it's hard to hide your own body," said the agent, threading his way over to Cathy. "It would be really hard to hide two bodies. Somebody somewhere would have found them."

"Not necessarily. They could have rented a motorboat,

149

driven out in the middle of some huge lake, fastened cement blocks to their own—"

"No," said Matt Keefer firmly. "Rory and Cade Lyman loved life. That's why they ran. They wouldn't love life in prison. They're out there somewhere doing fine."

Cathy's hands were trembling. She set them in her lap. They went on trembling. Shivers edged from her fingertips toward her elbows. Now her spine and her gut were shaking. They loved life, she thought. Not me.

Scootching his blue chair forward, Tommy Petrak slouched down over his knees, cupped his chin in his hands and took up a lot of space right in front of Cathy. Spencer, taking his cue, stretched his legs out and turned them into a big white sneaker fence.

Her cousin and her ride were trying to protect her. Tears sprang to her eyes. She could not let Matt Keefer see her weep. She drew the biggest breath her lungs allowed, picked up her lunch bag, looked way down, as if into a coal mine, and searched for food.

"Miss Ferris, I completely understand that you want to talk to your parents first. It's wise of you. If you'll give me their phone numbers, though, I'll call myself so they have the whole picture."

Why didn't he already have Marmee and Dad Bob's phone numbers? The source of those numbers—the headmaster—was across the room.

Cathy was not the sharpest knife in this particular kitchen. There were sixty other kids here who reached the same conclusion she did, only faster. Graydon said, "The headmaster refused to turn the phone numbers over to you? Go, Dr. Bella!" he called. "Privacy rights! I'm with you."

Ava said, "This puzzles me." She sounded as if being puzzled was a rare condition and she wasn't going to put up with it. "You're the FBI. You have to know where the real Murielle is. If she went into foster care, just go get her. If she's Cathy, you already know."

This time Matt Keefer was expressionless. He did it well.

It was Tommy who explained. "The FBI doesn't have access to records on Murielle. Five years ago they got so pushy demanding to interview my cousin during the first few days that Murielle stopped eating and she got very sick and had to be moved to a foster home, and right away to a second foster home. The Department of Children and Families said that a ten-year-old was too little to be interrogated, and when the FBI went to a judge for permission, they were turned down."

Cathy was as stunned as any of them.

Graydon said, "Murielle isn't ten anymore. Couldn't the FBI override that judgment now?"

"How do you know she's in foster care?" asked Meg. "My theory is that Rory and Cade came for Murielle. My parents would dismantle entire buildings to find me. I bet Murielle's parents would too. I bet she's with them."

Tommy had not taken his eyes off Cathy. He was not betting that Murielle was with her parents. He was betting that Murielle was sitting right next to him. His eyes were soft, as if the two of them had already discussed it.

Her stomach hurt, as if she were in the last stages of some awful cancer.

Cancer.

Was that this morning's phone call? Was it Marmee's doctor? Was the cancer back? Was Marmee sick?

"Later," Marmee had said.

With cancer, you did not always have a "later." How much time did they have? What would happen now? Surgery? Chemo?

A huge hole opened up in Cathy. Fear of cancer. The half of her that was Cathy wanted to run home, hug Marmee, be reassured that all was well.

"The state is still paying a stipend for Murielle's care," said Tommy.

"How'd you find that out?" asked Ava. "Whoever told you about the state money could tell you where Murielle is."

Tommy pointed to the FBI agent. "He was at our house last night. He's got a plan to flush Rory and Cade out of hiding. He wants to use Cathy's resemblance to Murielle to set up a sting."

A sting! The kids were equally shocked and thrilled.

Matt Keefer gave Tommy a look of mild displeasure.

Tommy said that for me, thought Cathy. He knows who I am. This is his gift. Here's what's coming, he's telling me. Do what you need to do.

But what did she need to do?

She didn't dare search further into the Mure Corporation, leaving an even longer virtual trail. She had no car in which she could drive to that Ansonia address and just ask the tenants where their landlords lived. She had no handy e-mail address for Rory and Cade. She never had had that. She had phoned and texted her parents a dozen times a day when she was little, but had rarely e-mailed.

I cannot warn them, thought Cathy.

A few feet away, Julianna Benner straightened. Her body became long and lean and alert.

I shouldn't warn them, either, thought Cathy. My parents deserve to get caught. They must be punished. My parents. Whom I love. They are bad.

The hole inside her deepened. She was falling down inside herself. Soon there wouldn't be a Cathy or a Murielle.

"What's the plan?" demanded Ava, eyes bright and face lifted in anticipation. "You're going to use Cathy as bait?"

"Thomas," said the agent warningly.

"You know what they're going to do, Tommy?" cried Ava. "Tell us. We'll keep it a secret. We won't tell anybody."

Sixty kids, thumbs poised, burst out laughing.

Tommy ignored them. He ignored Matt Keefer. He spoke only to Cathy. "They want you to pretend you're Murielle. They'll use photographs of you, Cathy, along with photographs my mother has of little Murielle. They'll use your voice. And of course your smile, because you look like Rory when you smile."

They would use her to seize Rory and Cade even when she *didn't* tell them anything.

"They'll put Murielle on YouTube or Facebook. Except you'll be Murielle. They'll give you a script to read," Tommy told her. "You'll pretend you have leukemia and you're dying. 'Mommy,' you'll say in your video. 'Daddy. Please come home. Please let me see you one last time.'"

· 17 ·

Murielle

There are questions with which everyone grapples.
Is there a God?

Who am I?

What will I do with my life?

With whom will I spend my life?

There was no knowing what Rory and Cade thought about God. But they had chosen each other, for better or for worse. And they had chosen money ahead of virtue.

Marmee and Dad Bob, whom she loved because they were kind and because she owed a great debt to them, felt close to God. They regarded God as an invisible neighbor who lived upstairs and could be counted on for advice and reassurance. They had chosen each other, and they had chosen jobs rather than careers. Their free time was not spent on travel or shopping or sports. It was given to other people's children.

And me? thought Murielle. How do I answer those questions?

Is there a God?

She remembered a church long ago, when there was nothing to be thankful for and she sat in a strange pew and wondered about God. For years Cathy had been likely to fold her arms in church and say silently to God: "I'm not impressed. You could have done better."

But perhaps God had done fairly well by Murielle Lyman.

For years Murielle had ached to be with her parents. It was physical. She imagined the loss of her parents as a jagged rock at the bottom of her lungs. Over time, the ache softened, and became more like fog, a cold bleak mist of the heart.

But all through it ran hope.

A few years ago, she had stumbled on a video when she was surfing the Web. It had been on television network news and found its way to all sorts of sites.

A navy ensign had been at war on the other side of the world. He'd been gone for seven months and his sudden return home was a complete surprise. He walked into his little son's first-grade class, and when the little boy saw him, the child flew across the room, crying, "Daddy! Daddy!" His father swept him up, holding him tight against his shoulder, where the little boy wept, and his father wept, and anybody watching it wept also.

She had watched it a hundred times.

When you don't have parents, wanting them back is the largest force in your life.

Thousands of times she had dreamed of such a hug. She could feel her feet pounding across the room, the joy rising from the bottom of her soul.

No such moment would happen. If Mommy and Daddy had planned to come home for a beautiful reunion, they would have been here by now. And now she was too old to fling herself across the room, a tiny body of pure joy, launching herself at her lost parents.

And now, in this student center, on display, in public, she faced the truth: her parents simply loved money more than they loved her.

Her parents had been in love with money—making it, spending it, investing it, manipulating it. To get that money, they had lied to clients, and when they had used up or lost their clients' money, they had grabbed what was left and they had run.

It wasn't freedom and it wasn't fear of prison that kept them hidden. It was the love of money.

Every year in church, there was bound to be a sermon dealing with the words of St. Paul, who said that the love of money is the root of all evil. Murielle even three days ago would not have said that her parents had done anything evil. But they had. They let Mrs. Benner go to prison for them.

If Rory and Cade had brought Murielle up, she would measure life by money.

Money was necessary, or there wasn't food on the table, heat in the house or shoes on the feet. But money was not a prime necessity. To love and to be loved headed that list. The love of Marmee and Dad was not the love of a real mommy and daddy. They weren't her birth parents. It was a decision. Like the love of God, it required nothing. All Cathy had to do was show up. And in the same way, she could have Aunt Lois's love. All Cathy had to do for that love was speak up.

But the love of her parents had been weak.

Who am I? was the second question.

All around her, kids were speculating about the very same thing. Who was she? Cathy Ferris, who happened to be the double of Murielle Lyman? Or Murielle?

I am both, she thought. I am not a double. I am two.

I am Murielle Catherine Lyman Ferris.

With whom will I spend my life?

The State of Connecticut had decided with whom she would spend her childhood. It had been in her power to telephone her aunt, but she hadn't. What combination of hurt and fear and confusion and helplessness had kept a little girl from trying? Or had it simply been conviction that Rory and Cade would be there any minute now?

What will I do with my life? Will I send my own parents to prison, which they deserve? Or will I help them escape, which my heart wants?

Parents were supposed to set the example. In Murielle's case, the example was: lie, steal, run, hide.

She imagined a recording studio where Matt Keefer would feed her lines: "Mommy! Daddy! I'm dying! Come get me!"

She imagined a drama coach demanding tears and a few sobs. She imagined that this could work. Even the most hardened parent would come to a hospital bed.

"Those poor parents!" said Spencer. "Imagine not knowing a single thing about your little girl for five years and then you find out she has leukemia and you rush to her bedside and it's all a scam and you're in jail."

Matt Keefer shook his head. "Whatever else the parents are, they're not poor. They have ten million dollars that we know about and probably a lot more we don't know about. And they are responsible for a fund so badly managed that they lost a hundred million that people entrusted to them."

"I think you should do it, Cathy," said Meg. "Think of the people who suffered. Or were punished. Like Julianna's family."

Nobody could look at Julianna and nobody could look away.

The FBI agent said sympathetically, "Did your family invest with the Lymans? Then you certainly know why we're doing this."

Julianna could have nodded and let the agent's attention return to Cathy. But she said, "My mother was the Lymans' office manager, Nancy Benner." She added, in front of every single classmate, "You sent her to prison."

The FBI did not send Nancy Benner to prison, thought Murielle. My parents did.

She saw Julianna as if through bars.

And Julianna Benner said, "I want you to do it, Cathy. I want them caught. I want them to pay."

There was still an entire afternoon of Latin to endure.

Endure. "To harden." From *durus,* "hard," or "lasting," as in "durable."

Mrs. Shaw explained the subjunctive mood. This was a method of conjugating a verb so that it described possible or hypothetical situations.

"Page one eighty-six, Wheelock," said the teacher. "*Hoc dicit ut eos iuvet.* 'He says this in order to help them.' It's in the subjunctive because it hasn't happened, but the

158

purpose is to make it happen. Next example. *Hoc facit ne capiatur.* 'He does this in order not to be captured.' Cathy, why is *capiatur* in the subjunctive in this example?"

Capio. "To take or seize." As in "capture." Her parents' fate existed even in a dead language.

Murielle could not speak.

Mrs. Shaw moved on. "Graydon?" she asked.

"Because it's a negative purpose clause."

I'll just quit summer school, thought Murielle. I don't know what's going on anymore anyway. I won't show up again, and somehow this will go away, and I won't have to be involved.

But she was not ten years old anymore. She was involved; she had to decide.

If she quit, she'd have to make more explanations than if she stayed. And it would not stop an FBI agent from pursuit. It would whet his appetite. All he had to do was get the word "Norwalk" from one student, and use a plain old phone book and find the only Ferris family in Norwalk, and he'd be at the Ferrises' before the Tartaglias brought her home.

During the afternoon break ("during"—also from *durus,* because it was both hard and lasting) Meg and Ava had argued about whether Murielle's parents had loved her.

Meg voted no. "Their poor little girl was an accessory, like designer shoes or scarves."

Listening to her classmates was like getting therapy by proxy. They were doing all the digging into her soul. She could just sit and listen.

"I say they did love her," argued Ava. "They thought

they'd left her safely with her aunt and uncle and her darling cousin Tommy, who is the most adorable boy in this whole summer school."

"Excuse me?" said Ethan. "Could you show a little loyalty to your fellow Latin scholars?"

Ethan was a shapeless boring big-nosed kid wearing a bad choice of glasses and sporting a difficult complexion.

Ava said, "Ethan, you are for sure in the adorable category, but Tommy is the overall winner." She spoke so seriously that Ethan sat taller, and suddenly was kind of attractive. Adorable was a stretch, but he might be adorable someday. He just had to leave age fifteen behind.

Colton was not interested in the adorable rankings. "Spencer, the guy that's Cathy's ride, thinks the Lymans are still in the U.S. If they are, they must have fake social security numbers. How do you get a fake social security number?"

"I read a mystery novel," said Meg, "where they found people who died young, took their social security numbers and became them and earned money as them."

"That is so icky," said Ava. "Hi, I'm a dead person."

They were all laughing, even Cathy.

"How do you find this dead person?" Ava asked. "They're dead. You can't meet them at a party."

There would be no escape from this kind of chatter. After school, since Mrs. Tartaglia had gone into the city today, Murielle and Spencer would have forty-five minutes to sit on that terrace, waiting for Spencer's father. She would be surrounded by people like Ava, stabbing her with questions. Matt Keefer might still be there, demanding ten minutes of her time.

Hysterical laughter began building in Murielle.

"What's funny?" asked Ava.

Nothing. There is nothing remotely funny in my life. I want to weep and rend my garments and tear my hair. I want to save my mother and father, but I want to do the right thing. How do you know what the right thing is? What do you do when two commandments bump into each other, so that if you honor your mother and father, you're helping them keep stolen goods?

"How come you're so into this, Ava?" Cathy asked.

"How come you're not?" Ava demanded.

"Everybody's placed bets, you know," said Graydon.

Ava stopped him. "Don't tell her. It's mean."

"There's a pool," said Graydon. "We all have money on it. Are you or aren't you Murielle Lyman?"

· 18 ·

Murielle

Once again down the vast solid stairs, through the big sterile student center, out the front hall and into the courtyard with its tall waving grass.

She felt as if she had emerged from prison. What a relief to be in the fresh air, the hot breeze, the sharp shadows, the wide sky. Prison must be so horrible. Even outside, you're in.

Matt Keefer was driving away.

She stared at the rear of his car, relieved and afraid. Where was he going? What did he know?

"You want to wait for my dad here or in the library?" asked Spencer. He wore high-top sneakers, which he must have bought yesterday, because they were perfectly white. Thick white socks reached up toward his knees. His khaki shorts had a wide turned-up hem. She kept her eyes at knee level, because she lacked the strength to meet the gazes of sixty kids listening in, hoping for more.

"This is fine." She found herself on the same circular

stone bench where she had sat that morning. Waving fronds of jungle grass brushed her back. The roar of departing cars comforted her. Her audience was diminishing.

But not by enough.

Tommy Petrak drew near. Julianna followed him.

The driver and passenger doors of an old sedan parked in a visitor slot opened. Lois and Travis Petrak got out. Lois straightened her clothes and patted her hair.

"I'm sorry, Cathy." Tommy's voice was almost inaudible. "My mother is desperate. She has to talk to you. Dad's along to help her chill. Believe me, she's not chilling. For five years, my mother has asked herself whether it would have been better if she'd taken Murielle to the airport after all, so the family could have fled together. I'm sure for Murielle it would have been better, because I think anything would be better than the foster system. But it wouldn't have been better for us. My mother would have been jailed. When they couldn't get at Rory and Cade, they wanted the next tier. They got Mrs. Benner. They were going to get us. The federal regulators were positive my parents knew the escape plan. They were at our house for days. Especially Agent Keefer. But also the National Association of Securities Dealers, the IRS, the U.S. Postal Inspection System, and the Securities and Exchange Commission."

Aunt Lois trudged across the bus lane, the bursting joy of yesterday gone. She looked heavy and worn.

Murielle felt as if her heart and Aunt Lois's were on crutches.

Uncle Travis was just a tall thin shape at her side. He did not seem to be a man upon whom Aunt Lois could lean. But then, I'm not a niece upon whom she can lean, thought Murielle.

"I could never tell," said Tommy, "whether the authorities genuinely thought my mother could find ten million dollars for them or whether they were having fun. Were they playing Let's Catch America's Most Wanted? My mother escaped being indicted as an accessory only because she didn't take you to the airport."

Tommy knew she was Murielle. She let it go. She had a thousand questions, and Lois Petrak could answer one or two of them.

Murielle stood up, walked forward and met Lois Petrak in the center of the courtyard. "Why did Rory do it?"

"Leave Murielle behind," asked Lois, "or take the money?"

"Start with the money."

"Rory was high-energy. She was always excited and busy and rushing and multitasking and planning and laughing. All that energy and exuberance swept people up, and everyone wanted to be part of her plans. I was lucky to be so much older, because if I'd been the younger one, I would never have measured up to a sister like Rory.

I've always thought Rory and Cade were having fun," Lois went on. "They loved risk. They entered the investing world during a decade when it was easy to make a fortune and the economy was roaring. Even the wildest risks were safe, and if they weren't safe, you could recover quickly. I think it was like bungee jumping for Rory. All those zeros to the left of the decimal point! They were hers! A million here, ten million there. Jump off the cliff with those dollars and see if you survive. I don't think my sister thought of what she did as stealing. She thought of it as shifting money so fast that so nobody could see. A high-speed game, a virtual-money game, poker with the highest stakes of all."

"No," said Uncle Travis, startling them both. "In poker, you play with your own money." He turned to Murielle. She shrank from his stare. Rory and Cade had damaged his family and he was still angry. "Rory was the smartest woman I ever met," said Uncle Travis, "and she understood with the first dollar she put into her own account instead of her client's that she was stealing. She could have pulled back. But she accelerated. She became a race car driver, reckless on the turns, not caring if the people behind her crashed and burned."

I crashed and burned, thought Murielle.

She remembered her last day in fourth grade, when everybody had looked at her so oddly. For the first time in all these years, she realized that their mothers and fathers had told them that Murielle's mommy and daddy were going to be arrested.

"And I didn't approve of how Rory raised her daughter," said Travis. "She and Cade left Muffin to the care of whatever babysitter showed up. They called the sitters au pairs and seemed to feel that using a French phrase made up for everything."

"Why are you still angry?" she whispered.

"Why? I loved Muffin. She was this darling, careful, disciplined, obedient little girl. She worked so hard to please parents who just weren't very interested."

But I still love them, she thought. I love them so. "What

do you think Rory and Cade are doing now?" she asked Aunt Lois.

"Having fun. I see them in Australia somehow. I'm not sure why. They were athletic. Australia's got a great climate. Perfect for people who don't have to work and need to fill time with some tough activity they can do over and over."

Life as an endless tennis game. Murielle put aside that vision. She felt ready now for the next question. Had Rory telephoned? "Hi, Sissy. Where's Murielle? I want to stop by and get her." Or maybe "Sissy, put Murielle on the phone." Or "How's Murielle doing in school? Does she still love purple?" Had Cade telephoned? "Okay, whatever, Lo. I don't care about what happened last time. Get her to the airport this time."

Murielle said to Lois, "Did Rory ever phone?"

"Six times. Always about Murielle. She said there had to be some way to get Murielle without attracting attention. I said I no longer had Murielle. Rory said get her back. I said if I knew how and where, I would."

"I was home for one of those calls," said her uncle. "I told Rory we could negotiate with the feds. Cut a deal. You surrender, Rory. In exchange, they let you see Murielle."

Rory had called six times. And six times, Lois, her sister, and Travis, her brother-in-law, had not turned her in.

All this time, Murielle had thought of them as the enemy. But it had never been true.

Murielle sensed motion behind her. Her classmates were drifting forward, trying to hear better.

"Rory was afraid," said Lois Petrak. "'I can't go to prison,' she kept saying. 'It's too scary and awful.' We sobbed on the phone because everything was scary and awful. But how much more scary and awful it must have been for Murielle."

Julianna Benner interrupted.

Murielle didn't want her here; didn't want any of them here; but who had more right to listen in than Julianna?

"Cathy," said Julianna, "I *want* things to be scary and awful for Rory and Cade Lyman. I don't care *who* you are. You can be *anybody*. For *any* reason. *I want Rory and Cade to get theirs.* Do the sting."

Murielle could not fill her lungs with air. Could not answer Julianna. Could no longer see her aunt and uncle.

"My dad's here," said Spencer loudly. "Hey, nice to talk to you, Mrs. Petrak. Got to run. Come on, Cathy. Bye, everybody. See you tomorrow." He set out at a jog, hauling Cathy along, pointing out the curb so she didn't trip.

"I forgot my book bag," she said numbly.

"I have it." He swung it up so she could see. They crossed the bus lane, crossed the grass, caught the car out on the road.

"Thank you for rescuing me, Spencer."

"Anytime. Cathy, this is insane. Tell your parents what is going on so they can put a stop to it. I feel for Julianna and everything, but you go on the Web as Murielle Lyman and you're there forever, and those Lymans and their crimes will stick to you."

———

Mr. Tartaglia was chatty and fun. Spencer gave him a rundown on the day's events, skipping Arabic and Latin in favor of the Lymans and the FBI.

Mr. Tartaglia was a more leisurely driver than his wife, slouching at the wheel, driving with the fingertips of one hand. They moved slowly up North Street, which was all mansions, all the time, a stunning series of immense beautiful homes, with beautiful trees and lawns that spread for acres, soft and velvet as putting greens, driveways with cobblestone aprons and stone walls capped by ornate iron fencing.

She now lived in a tougher town, a city less planned, less tended, less perfect.

A small white sign pointed to Stanwich Congregational Church. Just out of sight there would be a one-lane causeway over a small pond. Cars had to wait for opposing traffic. The church was elegant and symmetrical, with white clapboard and a slender spire. Even the parking lots were landscaped.

We all went to church, she thought. Every Sunday. How amazing.

"Do not store up treasures for yourselves on earth," Jesus said, *"but in heaven."*

No doubt Rory and Cade had listened to that verse. What had they thought as they carefully stored up treasures on earth? Not their own treasure either. Other people's.

Had they been amused by the thought of heaven? Had they said, "We'll worry about that later"? Or had they not been listening, just occupying a pew, enjoying the company, glad to dress up? Perhaps even using church to find clients.

168

"Pretend that you are dying of leukemia?" repeated Spencer's father. "That's low. And it doesn't sound right. How do you know this man is in the FBI?"

"Tommy knew him," said Spencer. "And Julianna remembered him."

"I don't like it. Cathy, do you want me to double-check this setup?"

"Dad," said Spencer, "that's for her parents to handle."

"Okay, fine. Cathy, hit me with some Latin. I was a Latin scholar once. *Amo, amas, amat. Amamus, amatis, amant.*"

"Outstanding," said Murielle. "How about *hic, haec, hoc*?" Will Matt Keefer be at my house when I get there? Will Marmee and Dad tell him, "Sure, look at the computer, we have nothing to hide."

"Oh, pronouns," said Mr. Tartaglia. "I think I never mastered those. I think it was a problem."

They talked languages the rest of the drive. It was like taking shelter.

Mr. Tartaglia refused to drop Cathy at the commuter lot. "I'm not in a hurry. I'd rather take you to your door. It sounds like you've had an exhausting day."

She didn't want them coming to her house. "Turn left," she said helplessly. "On Ten Rocks Road."

"And are there?" asked Mr. Tartaglia. "Ten rocks?"

"There's one in our front yard, anyway. It's a huge boulder dropped by the glacier. Great for playing on. Ledges and steps and craggy bits."

"I see it," called Spencer.

"That's a different one. Mine's another mile uphill."

"You've been walking home this whole way?" demanded Mr. Tartaglia.

169

"It's not that far. Here's my house."

How small and shabby it looked after the mansions of Greenwich. She could feel Mr. Tartaglia biting back an exclamation. "It isn't Greenwich, is it?" she acknowledged. "It probably isn't Wilton, either. But it's a nice place to live. Thanks for the ride, Mr. Tartaglia. Thanks for the rescue, Spence. I'll see you tomorrow."

But Spencer got out of the car too.

She looked at him.

He flushed. He touched his hair. Pulled at the collar of his polo shirt. Sighed.

What did Spencer have to be nervous about? She was the one with the nightmare. She walked slowly toward her house. He walked with her. His new white sneakers seemed to tangle.

"I thought I might have a pool party on Saturday," Spencer croaked. "Dad knows where you live now, so he and I can come and get you and then bring you home again. Want to come?"

He *was* nervous. He was afraid she would say no. Which meant that her answer mattered. Which meant that he liked her.

For one beautiful moment, she was neither Cathy nor Murielle. She was just a girl smiling at a boy. "I'd love to."

· 19 ·

Murielle

Murielle went straight to the refrigerator.

Being asked to a pool party was not a carrot-stick moment. Not a leftover-pizza moment. Not a hard-boiled-egg moment. She shut the refrigerator door and opened the freezer. Half a chocolate layer cake looked up at her from beneath its clear plastic wrap. She took it out, peeled off the plastic gently so it wouldn't tear the icing, set it in a sunny spot to defrost, and poured herself a glass of milk. It tasted so good.

I won't think about Rory and Cade now, she told herself. I'll have cake. Later is fine for Rory and Cade.

Maybe Marmee will let me buy a new bathing suit. I don't actually need one. But a pool party . . .

It was nice to concentrate on something shallow instead of something huge and profound.

Marmee's car pulled in. She was alone. Jamesy was not in the car. How strange. Dad Bob must be picking him up. But today Dad Bob had bowling.

Marmee got out of the car slowly and seemed to drag herself toward the house.

Murielle remembered the phone call. Had it been the doctor? Was the cancer back? Had Marmee left Jamesy in day care so she could have a few minutes to cry? Dad Bob would never go bowling again; he'd be nursing his dying wife.

Murielle threw the door open. "Marmee?"

Marmee did not smile reassuringly. She dropped her purse and tote bag on the floor, which she never did; anything on the floor Jamesy regarded as his property. She gripped the barstool and slowly slid on, staring blankly at the cake. There were tear tracks on her cheeks. "Jamesy's gone. The caseworker came and got him."

Jamesy was gone?

"Jamesy's mother did well in rehab. She learned some vocational skill in prison. They think she'll stay off drugs this time. She wanted her son back. So he was returned to his mother."

"Returned to his mother" was such a beautiful phrase. Except that Jamesy's mother used cocaine, a habit she could not surrender very long. She would forget her little boy. She had left him alone and without food many times.

"That was the phone call this morning? And the arguing last night?" How could so much happen at the same time? Why wasn't it spread evenly over the years, like butter on toast? Why were there dry months with nothing happening and then a single day sopping with emotion?

Marmee nodded. "The social workers have been talking about it, but his mother hasn't managed to be a parent before and I didn't see any evidence that she would this time. I was sure they'd decide against it. I dropped Jamesy off at day care, and I was driving into the hospital parking lot when they called to say they'd pick Jamesy up after his nap."

"You didn't get to say good-bye?"

"I took a personal day. I drove straight home and packed his things. Then I rushed over to the day care and played with him until they came, and I told him how I love him, and how Dad loves him, and you love him, and how wonderful he is, and how wonderful that he and Mama are going to be together again. I said, 'You give Mama a kiss for me.' We practiced giving a kiss to Mama."

"What did Jamesy say?"

"He's four. What does he know at four? He said, 'Okay.'"

But was it okay? Jamesy aroused bad temper in practically everybody. Jamesy's mother was known for her bad temper.

No point in eating, not even chocolate cake, because food couldn't fill the hollow that was in Murielle. "If it doesn't work out, do we get him back?"

"Probably not."

"I didn't get to say good-bye."

"That's just as well. 'Good-bye' is a terrible word. Jamesy is too little to understand."

Saying good-bye to your family is something nobody can understand, no matter what age they are. I will never understand my parents, she thought.

She had a sudden piercing knowledge that Julianna Benner was lucky. No matter how bad the situation, Julianna did not lose her mother and now her mother was back home. Things were dark, but the four Benners were together.

Marmee made a pot of strong coffee and sipped while she talked on the phone to her own mother, her mother-in-law, her sister and her best friend.

Murielle folded laundry. Matching socks took all her strength.

Jamesy's mother, in spite of addiction and jail and poverty and failure, had not abandoned her child. She was going to try again to be a mom.

But Murielle's parents had never tried again.

Murielle took the folded laundry upstairs. She peeked into Jamesy's room.

Toy trucks and cardboard building blocks, action figures and stuffed animals were strewn around, waiting for a child who would not play with them again. For the first time in years, she pictured her own bedroom: the covers she never again pulled back and the bed she never again slept in. The clothes in the closets, the beloved books and toys and dolls. The souvenirs, framed photographs, bracelets, shoes. What had happened to them?

When she arrived at the Ferrises', this crib, chest of drawers and toy box had been here. There had been other foster children Jamesy's age before she arrived. There would be more later. She and Jamesy were part of a cycle. These amazing people, her foster parents, would dry their tears one morning and call social services, and say that they were ready for another child.

Downstairs, Marmee yelled, "Phone for you!"

Matt Keefer must have gotten the number. He—

"It's Grammy!"

Murielle picked up the phone. "Hi, Grammy," she said to her foster mother's mother.

"Oh, darling girl, I'm heartbroken about Jamesy. Thank goodness we still have you. But I hardly see you anymore, you're so busy. Tell me about summer school, sweetheart. How is Latin?"

"It's good. I'm good at it. How was your bridge tournament? Did you whip everybody?"

"No. We were average," said Grammy. "I hate being average. I mean, what's the point? You should always be a winner, right?"

Very soon, maybe tomorrow, thought Murielle, I won't be average anymore. But I won't be a winner, either. Whether I want to or not, I'll be bait.

Ava's opinion of the leukemia plan was that it was disgusting, sick, mean and probably workable. She polled her family. Her own four adults —mother and stepfather, father and stepmother—rarely agreed on anything, which was handy, because it gave so much balance to discussions.

Her mother was practical. "Cathy Ferris's parents won't allow it. Once you have photographs on the Web, they're there forever. They won't permit their child to be portrayed as somebody else, especially somebody dying, and furthermore, the child of criminals."

Her stepfather was skeptical. "People like Rory and Cade Lyman, they've got to be careful three hundred sixty-five days a year, twenty-four hours a day. They're not going to fall for this. All they do is use another prepaid disposable cell phone, call this Cathy up, ask some question about her supposed childhood, and they'll know she's a fake."

At her other house, however, her father was fascinated. "I think it's brilliant. They should try it. If ever a pair of crooks should be in jail, it's the Lymans."

Her stepmother, Kay, was sad. "I don't think the Lymans meant to be crooks. I think they meant to be captains of investment. I think sudden drops in the economy caused their fund to sink and they panicked and tried to shift stuff around and stay afloat, and believed they could pay it back before anybody caught on. I don't think they meant to rip people off."

Her father said, "Kay. Get a life. They're scum."

Ava retreated to her room and prepared for a long evening. Ava hardly ever went to bed before midnight and was often up at one or two. Sure, she was tired in the morning, but so was everybody. You had to squash it all in somehow, and night was a flexible time. Every now and then, one of her four parents asked her not to stay up, but she never paid any attention.

This guy Keefer was old. Ava bet he didn't understand the Internet and wasn't going to use it right. He perceived the Web as a glowing, quick-change, online newspaper or TV station. Ava bet that the Lymans, who must have lived in front of their computers, keeping track of stocks and whatever, knew how teenagers communicate.

In her opinion, the leukemia thing was overkill. You didn't need it. Ava could do it just as easily, skip the leukemia, make Julianna happy and take a load off Cathy's shoulders.

Unless she was Murielle. In which case, she should have said so.

Ava IM'ed Tommy Petrak. "I need photographs of Murielle when she was ten plus the photographs you took of Cathy. I want to enlarge them to study the bone structure." Ava was good at fibbing.

"Leave the poor girl alone," he wrote back. "I was a jerk and now we're in yet another mess and my mother is frantic all over again."

"What if you weren't a jerk? What if she is Murielle? Don't you want to know?"

"Are you a specialist in bone structure?"

"Just humor me, okay?"

He humored her.

Ava was slightly shaken by the photos of little Murielle. Such a sober child.

Then she shrugged.

The FBI was searching for the parents. But it was more logical to search for Murielle. Most kids had an online presence. She checked YouTube, MySpace, Tangle, Facebook, Flickr. No Murielle Lyman. Ava checked Cathy/Catherine Ferris. There were several with that name, but since ages were listed upfront, she could tell they were too old.

It was a little surprising that Cathy Ferris had no online presence. She knew from lunch talk (pre–Murielle sighting) that Cathy was on her own high school's tennis and field hockey teams. Her friends surely exchanged photos of games and successes and possible boyfriends standing in the crowd.

She tried people-search engines for Murielle Lyman.

177

Nice that both her names were so unusual. But she found nothing.

If Rory and Cade were out there hoping to find a trace of their daughter, they had a routine. If they were not running frequent searches, nothing short of headline news on network television would catch their eye. Maybe not even then, if they were in some hole like Namibia. Not that Ava believed for one minute that people who used to live in North Greenwich would bolt to a place that didn't get television, Internet or cell phone reception.

Murielle's coming soon to a space near you, Rory, Ava said silently. Ready or not, Cade, real or not, Cade, your daughter's here.

It was like a death in the family. Everybody the Ferrises knew came and they all brought food.

Marmee's sister drove over with her daughter, who was twenty-five, and Grammy and Grampa came over, and there were lasagna and chicken-broccoli casserole and apple crisp, and everybody sat around the table and had chocolate cake and coffee and told stories. First the stories were about Jamesy, and then they were just stories, to prove there was love in the house, and history, and a future.

The relatives had half forgotten that Cathy too was a foster child. After nearly five years, she was theirs.

She wondered if Matt Keefer's plan would work. Rory and Cade could decide not to come, even to see a dying daughter. They might prefer the beach where they frolicked, the clubs where they partied. Maybe they had half forgotten Murielle; would just roll over on the sand where they were catching a few rays and make sure they tanned evenly. Or maybe they never bothered with the Web, or spoke another language now, or were busy with other, younger children.

She thought of these phantom brothers and sisters.

She doubted their existence. Nobody with a screaming two-year-old, say, was invisible. On the other hand, what better camouflage for a jet-set couple than to become dowdy middle-aged parents changing diapers?

"Penny for your thoughts, Cath," said Grampa. "You haven't heard a word we've been saying."

"I'm enjoying it, though. I'm sort of basking in how you're here."

Marmee burst into tears. "I don't know if Jamesy is okay." Her family embraced her.

Mommy, thought Muriclle, are you weeping for me? Are you out there somewhere wishing you could sit at the table with me, and comfort me?

Ava decided on MySpace. She chose two of Tommy's pictures of Murielle as a child. She added the photograph she had taken of Cathy on her cell phone, and then the photos collected from other kids in summer school. There was even a seven-second video of Tommy kneeling while Cathy stared at him.

She composed a letter from Murielle to the missing parents. She added music, gave Murielle a hobby and a favorite quote, and sent it out into the world.

It was two a.m.

Before Ava started her Latin, she checked an international clock.

If Rory and Cade were in London, it was already seven a.m. They might be having tea and preparing to read the first bits of morning news. If they were in Hong Kong, it was two p.m. tomorrow, a perfect time to snuggle up in front of the computer. Los Angeles, it was only eleven tonight. They had probably wrapped up for the day.

Who knew when Rory and Cade would sit in front of their computer and search once again for Murielle?

It could be a week. It could be a month.

It could be now.

· 20 ·

Murielle

In the morning, Marmee drove her to the commuter lot. They didn't talk. Too much emotion and too little sleep. Marmee wrongly assumed that her foster daughter was emotional about the same things she was.

"Bye, Marmee. Try to have a good day."

"You too, honey," said her mother wearily.

In the car, Mrs. Tartaglia told New York City stories while Spencer and Murielle sat in the back, strapped down with two feet of upholstery between them, like strangers on a train. Happiness sifted through Murielle's anxieties. Spencer liked her.

When Spencer's mother ran out of stories, Murielle said softly, "Who else is coming to the pool party, Spencer? Who else did you ask from summer school?"

"Um. Only you."

"And everybody else is from Wilton?"

"Um. No. There is no everybody else. Actually, it's kind of a stretch to call it a pool party. I have a pool. But—well, the party is just us. I was thinking we could just—well, you know. Swim."

"In the olden days," said Mrs. Tartaglia, "we called it a date. Boys today are very shy."

"Mo-om," said Spencer.

"You'll be chaperoned, Cathy," added Mrs. Tartaglia. "I live by the pool."

"Mo-om."

"It sounds perfect," said Murielle. Perfect, except Spencer had asked a girl named Cathy and today he might well learn that she didn't exist. And would the girl named Murielle be able to go to his house on Saturday or would she be busy with the FBI?

Mrs. Tartaglia said, "Spence told me what the FBI wants to do, Cathy. It's totally sick. Pretend to die of leukemia so that Murielle's parents come out of the woodwork? As if Rory and Cade were termites?"

The kids laughed. They were still laughing when they got out of the car at Greenwich High and walked in together. There was no sign of Matt Keefer or the headmaster. The students had not gathered in little knots to discuss Murielle Lyman. It was an ordinary school day, a little hotter than most. The air-conditioning was barely on, because there were barely any people in the building.

"See you at lunch," said Spencer. He sort of waved.

"See you at lunch." She sort of reached for his fingertips and then floated up the concrete stairs. Tucking the happiness back inside, because she wasn't ready to share it yet, she braced herself for Ava, Meg, Julianna, Ethan, Colton and Graydon. They were going to be studying her as well as Latin.

During break, however, they talked about major-league baseball. Ethan, Julianna and Meg were ardent Yankees fans. Colton favored the Mets. Ava thought baseball was stupid. Graydon was a Red Sox man. It began to look as if they would have to reseat the class based on this new knowledge.

When it was time for lunch, Murielle realized that she had forgotten to pack one. It had been that kind of morning. Of course, now that there was no food available, she was starving and would have eaten anything. "Does anybody have extra lunch?" she asked. "Even a crust? Or a single potato chip?"

Everybody had extra lunch. Offers came from all sides. They thundered down the stairs, as if there were dozens of Latin students, not just seven.

"Ava!" hollered Meg. "Hurry up!"

"I have to check something on my laptop."

"Ava has a laptop?" said Graydon. "I thought she used a BlackBerry Curve."

"She likes the bigger screen when she checks her Facebook stuff," said Meg.

They were the last class into the student center.

Spencer was already sitting at the Latin table. Tommy was there too. Murielle checked all four walls and every entrance. No Agent Keefer.

But Lois and Travis Petrak were standing under the cardinal flag. Oh, no! Were they going to come every day? She couldn't let this go on. It had to be resolved. *She* had to resolve it.

Aunt Lois came forward in a big heavy way, like a truck maneuvering. "I'm not going to let them do this horrible publicity they have in mind. I'm here to stop it from happening."

What am I afraid of? If ever two people can take care of themselves, it's Rory and Cade. It's my aunt who needs me. *I* need me! I need to be Murielle!

"Guess what!" shrieked Ava from the top of the stairs. She wasn't visible yet. Her voice echoed against all the stone. Sixty kids looked up. Ava whirled down the circular stairs, shouting, "They answered! I set up a MySpace page for Murielle Lyman and they answered! Rory and Cade wrote back!"

Murielle was blind, deaf and mute.

She was all hope and all horror.

They answered?

Ava held up her laptop as if it were a trophy at a horse race, pivoting like a model on a runway to give everybody a view of a screen instead of a hemline. " 'Dear Mure,' " Ava read. " 'We are filled with hope. Can it be you? Your photograph makes us weep with joy. You look like such a wonderful young woman. Tell us everything. Love, Mommy and Daddy.' "

Murielle was on her feet, feeling her way around the table, tears streaming down her face. Nobody ever called her Mure except her parents. She never called her parents anything except Mommy and Daddy.

Why didn't *I* do this? thought Murielle. Why didn't *I* look for them? Why was it always *their* responsibility to find *me*? I was a partner! Why didn't I even try? Why is it *Ava* who sent them a message?

They were bad parents, but what kind of daughter was I?

I was the kind of daughter who gladly became another person.

Ava set the laptop down on the Latin lunch table. Murielle wiped away the flooding tears and looked down at the screen.

Dear Mure,

We are filled with hope. Can it be you? Your photograph makes us weep with joy. You look like such a wonderful young woman. Tell us everything.

Love, Mommy and Daddy

Her lips moved as if she were just learning to read, or as if a message from her parents was yet another foreign language. Her hands were so cold and stiff, she was not sure she could use the keyboard. But nothing mattered now except knowing. Was it really Rory? Was it really Cade?

She typed.

Dear Mommy and Daddy,

What did you put in my backpack that day?

Love, Murielle

She had never heard the kind of silence she was hearing in the student center now. It was the silence of not breathing, not talking, not shuffling, not chewing.

It was the silence of waiting.

She was trembling so hard now that she seemed to have palsy.

She stared at the screen.

Mommy and Daddy were sitting together somewhere. Perhaps they were holding hands. Perhaps they were praying. Perhaps their eyes were glued to the electronic rectangle that would give them back their little girl.

It seemed to her that she waited another five years, all of it in the thick waiting silence of stares, and then came the reply.

The words leaned in and out, changing shape under her tears.

Ava could not resist the drama. Leaning over Murielle, she read the answer out loud.

" 'Dear Murielle,' " said Ava in ringing tones. " 'It was a pink backpack with silver stripes. Inside were a cell phone, ten one-hundred-dollar bills, a new hoodie, a Little House book and some snacks. We love you. Please tell us if you've been all right. Love, Mommy and Daddy.' "

If I've been all right? thought Murielle. Who are these people who wonder if their baby girl has been all right when she didn't have her parents?

Ava, Spencer and every single other kid in the student center held a phone in one hand. They were texting. Except for Julianna Benner. She held a small white business card. She was not texting. She was dialing. "Mr. Keefer?" she said.

I was right, thought Tommy Petrak. I opened the flip top of my soda can, turned to speak to a friend and there was Murielle across the room. I was on my feet, staggering toward her, calling her name! I'm Cathy, she kept saying. You're Murielle, I kept saying.

And I was right.

He looked at this girl who was not really Murielle at all but another person named Cathy, and he wondered how she had gotten there, and whether it was good. He looked at her tears, and he knew that she loved her mother and father.

It was comforting. What matters, really, except family? And hers was bad, and had left her behind, but she still loved them.

His anger at Rory and Cade softened for a moment, while he saw the extent of Muffin's love, and then his anger surged back, twice as large, a tsunami of anger.

How dare they!

He did not for one moment believe that Rory and Cade would appear. When they fled, the media treated them almost as cowboys, riding off into the sunset after their daring bank robbery. But now, with the national economy in tatters, they were symbols of bad judgment, of a sick appetite for insane risk and, most of all, symbols of raw greed. If they came back now, they'd go to prison for decades. Or be strung up by a lynch mob.

The anger ebbed away once more.

He saw only his cousin.

Would Murielle let him be family? Would she let his mother be her aunt? Would she let them bring her home?

Julianna pitied Cathy. Cathy's parents were so rotten that Cathy, even at ten, had known she had to be somebody else. And now Ava had trapped her. Cathy had no escape, any more than Julianna had had an escape.

Pray pray pray that Rory and Cade had no escape.

"Right now," she said to Matt Keefer. "Live. Real time.

You can trace them somehow, I know you can." She elbowed Ava and Tommy out of her way and gave Matt Keefer the details he needed to see the same screen wherever he was.

Julianna felt shivers from the crowd of kids and knew that they were not on her team, but on Cathy's. Murielle's.

She didn't care. There was a chance to make Rory and Cade pay, and she would do anything in her power to make that happen.

Ava had been having fun. She was the youngest student in summer school, and had just become the most powerful. She herself had located Rory and Cade and unmasked Cathy Ferris.

The wrath in Julianna's voice stopped Ava cold.

Who am I? thought Ava.

A good citizen, locating criminals and working for justice?

Or an interfering gossipy lowlife, feasting on the troubles of classmates?

Relief billowed over and around Lois Petrak, like sheets on a clothesline in a wind. She lifted her face to the breeze of knowing—knowing at last—that Muffin was all right. She, Lois, had not done irrevocable harm to her little niece. Her little niece had grown into a bright, beautiful, courteous and tough young woman.

Muffin loved her mommy just as Lois Petrak loved her sister.

And hated her too, no doubt. Or she would have made an effort long ago to find her parents herself.

Why was she here at Greenwich High? What had she wanted? How had she become Cathy Ferris?

Would she tell her aunt?

Would she say, Yes, I'm Murielle, Aunt Lois. Yes, I love you.

Spencer thought, She's a double. Literally. She's both Murielle and Cathy.

He felt oddly sick, watching her as if she were an exhibit. She had just become a stranger to him. He did not know what to think of the pool party. He had been so eager to invite her over; so anxious about it; so worried because he had to have his parents' knowledge and cooperation and he didn't really want them to be part of it, but he had no other way to get her to his house, and now he didn't really know who it was that he had found so intoxicating.

Not that it mattered.

A lot of people were going to want Murielle-Cathy tomorrow. A pool party would be struck from the list. She would be talking to lost relatives and to the FBI.

Her tears had stopped. She had come to a decision. She lifted her hands to type.

What will she write? he wondered. What would I write?

But his ordinary life, with his ordinary parents, had nothing in common with the lives of Murielle and Cathy.

The tears welled over and ran down her cheeks, soft and warm and itchy. She stared through them.

They betrayed me. But I betrayed them. I threw away the name Murielle. I threw away the name Lyman. I never called my aunt Lois, sister of my mother, the grown-up to whom my parents entrusted me. I never tried to get back to the home where my mother expected to find me. I know how to use the Internet as well as Ava. I looked for news about whether my parents were arrested, but I never did what Ava did. I never shouted all over the world, Here I am!

I hid as well as Rory and Cade hid, thought Murielle.

Somebody was sobbing.

It might be her aunt.

I'm so cruel, thought Murielle. I let go of my aunt, who loved me. I was only ten, but I had power and I used it.

I'm fifteen now. I still have power. I can still use it.

A few feet away, Julianna snapped her cell phone closed as if it were a guillotine on the necks of Rory and Cade.

But no matter how fast the FBI moved, unless Rory and Cade Lyman had lost their touch, they could just melt away and vanish once again.

What did she want most in the world? To see her parents? Or have them safe?

Should she write "Come"?

Or should she write "Go"?

· 21 ·

Murielle

There was so much that Murielle ached to know. *Why?* Where are you? What do you look like? What life do you lead? There was so much she wanted to share with her parents—the autobiography of five lost years.

But there was no time to exchange a single syllable. Matt Keefer would already be reading this same screen and notifying FBI computer experts, who would begin a search for the fugitives.

Fugitives who needed to be punished. Fugitives who had hurt individuals and even their country by their theft. Fugitives who must be brought to justice.

She saw Justice standing there, robed and carved of stone. Justice, whose stern face never showed emotion.

But these fugitives were the mother and father of Murielle Lyman, who was neither stern nor stone.

She could never wrap a present or give a kiss to this mother and father. She would never share a joke with them or fix a meal. She did not even have time to say she loved them. They would have to deduce it from the message she sent. She must give them an order. It must be very clear. "Come." . . . or "Go."

They love me, she thought, but not enough to come back. They never loved me enough to come back. That's what I've been hiding from. Cathy Ferris was my cover, so I would never have to admit it. Starting with that social worker long ago, and the other three foster children in that first home—Latisha and Luke and Raphael—and ending with every kid standing in this student center, they all knew the truth. When they look at me, they think: *Her parents don't love her enough to come back*.

And I must have have known too. Not at first, not for months; but later. That's why, over the years, they ceased to be Mommy and Daddy in my mind and became Rory and Cade.

How much do I love them? How much do I love justice?

I can't have both.

The right thing is justice. But the other thing is love. Rory and Cade are Mommy and Daddy. And there is one gift I can give them.

Permission.

Murielle Catherine Lyman put her fingers on the keyboard of Ava's laptop and typed. She didn't write "Come" and she didn't write "Go." There was another word, a sharper word, which would tell them that danger was at hand.

The daughter of Rory and Cade Lyman wrote in caps:

RUN.

In a perfect world, Murielle would have handled this nightmare in private. But the world occupied by Murielle Lyman was not perfect. She had sixty witnesses.

"'Run'!" Ava was crying incredulously. "She told her parents to run!"

"'Run'!" they all repeated, as if this were a foreign word, in one of their languages, a difficult word that nobody could have expected.

Murielle clicked Send. The message flew to its unknown destination. She broke the Internet connection, shut down the computer and closed the laptop. A shiver coursed through her. It wasn't fear or grief.

She had set herself free.

Rory and Cade could override the instruction to run. They could return and stand in front of Justice. But they wouldn't. They would always be caught in their own trap. Not a prison; in no way equivalent to a prison. And yet, they were not free.

Oh Rory, oh Cade, thought their daughter. You have so much to answer for. Maybe I let you go not for your sake. Maybe I let you go for my sake, so that I never have to tell you what I think of you. So that I don't have to be Cathy anymore, that pleasant person nobody knows, living in a house chosen by the state.

"Cathy, you warned them?" shouted Julianna.

"I had to. They're my parents."

"They're criminals who deserve punishment, Cathy!"

"Yes. But I'm not Cathy. I'm Murielle. You were my example, Julianna. You stuck by your mother. I have to stick by mine."

193

Julianna was furious. "Your parents did literally ten million times more damage than my mother."

"I know that. I apologize for what they did."

But an apology does not make up for a prison sentence, especially when Murielle had probably saved Rory and Cade from their prison sentences. Julianna did not waste another second. She opened her cell phone and touched Redial. In a moment, she would be talking to Matt Keefer.

Murielle wished that she did not have to hear. She looked the other way and there stood her cousin. Tommy was not smiling. It wasn't an occasion for smiling. If she had admitted that yes, she was Murielle, at that moment when he was full of joy and crying her name, what a celebration there would have been. The lost was found! Muffin was home!

But she had remained in hiding and now was aiding and abetting criminals who had brought suffering to the Petraks. "I'm sorry, Tommy. When you came over to me, I wasn't ready. I didn't expect you to know me. I said the wrong things."

Tommy looked sad. Because she'd protected Rory and Cade? Or because she hadn't bothered with her aunt Lois and her uncle Travis and her cousin Tommy all these years? "It's okay," he said, as if he weren't so sure. "I'm just glad we found you. But why are you here? Why did you come, if you weren't going to admit that you're Murielle?"

The summer school students hung on every word. The truth would have to be public property. "I think maybe I came to stand on the edge of the life I should have led," Murielle told him. "Look in. See if you were still here."

"I've been mad at Rory every day for five years," said Aunt Lois.

Murielle had forgotten her aunt, who was only a few rows of kids and a dozen steps away. "Now I'm even madder," said Lois. "Stand on the edge of life? I never heard anything so awful. Life is for jumping in."

How they had damaged each other: the middle-aged aunt, the ten-year-old who had been Muffin and the fifteen-year-old who was Cathy.

No, thought Murielle. My aunt did the right thing—she kept me from being a fugitive. I alone caused the damage.

It was like being thrown into ice water.

"I'm sorry," she cried out, her voice breaking. "I'm sorry I didn't ever call you up, Aunt Lois. I'm sorry I didn't hug you when you stood there in the courtyard."

Aunt Lois held out her arms. Murielle walked into her aunt's embrace. She could feel her aunt's heartbeat.

"Muffin, honey, you have nothing to be sorry for. The grown-ups in your life made mistakes and you paid." She took Murielle's face in her hands and kissed her cheeks. "Welcome home."

Murielle—who had gladly vanished into somebody named Cathy—was going to get a welcome home?

"You'll live with us now," said her aunt decisively. "I need you. I've needed you for five years, Muffin. We love you."

She had an aunt who loved her.

A cousin who had knelt at her feet, begging her to exist.

An uncle who had once thought that little Murielle was perfect.

Rory and Cade had almost crushed the Petrak family,

and Murielle had hurt them every day she failed to call, and still, they wanted her home.

I have a real family, she thought.

Marnie and Bob Ferris became smaller and less important.

They won't be surprised, thought Murielle. It's what a foster parent learns. You love while you can and then you give the child back. How brave! Could I be that brave? It's a hundred times braver than my parents ever were. "I need you too, Aunt Lois. I can't wait to come home."

Murielle exhaled, as if she had been holding her breath for years.

Whatever Rory and Cade Lyman had done to others still existed, was still wrong, should still be punished. But what Rory and Cade had done to her was over.

Julianna's harsh voice pierced the hush. "You find them, Matt Keefer!" she said fiercely into her phone. They all heard the snap of its tiny lid as she closed it.

Murielle forced herself to look at the crowd. Sixty kids looked back. Whose side were they on? Or were they just soaking up a circus act? Toward the back towered Spencer, his long chaotic hair protecting his expression, and rows of spectators protecting his position.

A voice came from the top of the stairs. "Didn't you hear the bell? We have a tight schedule, you know. Kindly get to class."

Spencer was the first to leave. Only to Murielle did this matter. In everybody else's mind, Spencer was just her ride. When he pivoted and took a step toward his hallway, his tall body was like an instruction. The students followed his example, and headed for class.

She croaked, "Spencer?"

He paused. He turned, but not enough to face her; just enough to acknowledge her. "You probably won't need a ride home today," he said, not joking. "I'll explain it to my mother."

The other kids had no interest in car pool details. They burst into talk, sharing every thought before they had to speak in foreign languages about less interesting things.

The students reached the halls and stairs, and vanished from sight. Tommy, Murielle and Aunt Lois remained in place, like actors on an abandoned stage. Across the room, framed against stacked tables, Spencer waited.

"I thought I was Cathy," she told him. "But Murielle is who I am. I don't know if Murielle is very likeable. I hardly know Murielle myself. But I still want us to be friends." She wanted to be more than friends. "Can I still come to the pool party, Spencer? Even if I'm somebody else?"

The headmaster loped into the student center, holding up his cell phone. He frowned at Spencer. "Please go straight to class," said Dr. Bella. "Mrs. Petrak, it seems your cell phone is turned off. I have Agent Keefer on my phone."

Spencer didn't move.

Aunt Lois took Dr. Bella's phone. "Muffin, honey, I'll just say hello to Matt, and then you and I are going out for lunch. Tommy, do you want to join us or go to class? There's a lot to say, but we don't have to say everything now. Spencer, I know you only as Muffin's ride. You seem to be something more. I'd be glad to have you at lunch too."

Spencer shook his head. "Thanks, but I can't afford to

skip class. And I think her weekend is going to be too busy for swimming."

Her weekend. She was just a pronoun now.

But—he was still standing there.

"I was going to buy a new bathing suit," she told him.

He grinned suddenly, and flung back the mop of excess hair, and she caught a brief glimpse of his entire face. It was a nice one. "Maybe some other Saturday, then." He took a step toward his classroom, turned again and added, "Maybe you did the right thing. I like to think I'd do anything for my parents. But maybe not. Your situation is too crazy for me."

"It's crazy for me too, Spence," said Tommy, "and I'm part of it. Muffin, I'm going to class. Not that I'll learn any Chinese. I'm pretty strung out. But Mom's been waiting for you for five years. You two talk. Maybe I'll see you for supper. Or maybe your foster parents—wow—what about them?"

Marmee and Dad Bob were going to be the easy ones.

The tough questions were in this room.

Would she have friends after this awful beginning? What about her friends in Norwalk? Could she stay in summer school? Should she drop out for Julianna's sake? Would Spencer like her as Murielle?

Tommy and Spencer jogged off to class.

They're glad to get out of here, she thought. Way too much emotion in this room.

Aunt Lois spoke into the headmaster's cell phone. "Hello, Matt," she said, as if they were old friends. Perhaps they were; perhaps five years of being antagonists and afraid of or furious with each other had created a

198

weird friendship. "I'm going to take my niece out for lunch, and then I'll meet with you. In the meantime, you can probably talk to Ava—I don't know her last name—and see how she pulled this off, and what details she can give you. Don't yell at me, Matt. And when we get together, don't yell at my niece, either. Do I need to have a lawyer and should Murielle's foster parents be there, or are you going to behave?"

Murielle heard Matt Keefer say, "I'm not the one with the behavior problems."

She suddenly giggled, and remembered that he had been kind when her parents vanished. He had never questioned her roughly; he had just questioned her, which he'd had to do. And she had stayed silent, which she'd had to do.

Aunt Lois handed the phone to Dr. Bella, and he went back to his office. They stood, aunt and niece, in the huge empty student center, under the flags and the banners.

"What kind of restaurant do you like?" asked her aunt.

"Aunt Lois, I don't want to go to a restaurant. I want to go home. Can we just go home and have a sandwich?"

"Oh, Muffin! I can't think of anything better than to bring you home."

We'll laugh, thought Murielle. We'll say terrible things about Rory and Cade—we who are the only two people on earth who still love them. We'll talk about justice and whether it will ever come to them and how Matt Keefer will deal it out to us. We'll call Marmee and Dad, and Uncle Travis.

And then we'll have dessert. Something rich and sweet, after all that dark and difficult talk.

As for Rory and Cade, I will never know if there is anything sweet in their lives, or if they are rich in anything besides money.

But I will have two riches: forgiveness and family.

Murielle walked out of the high school with her aunt Lois.

Three riches, she thought, smiling at her aunt. I am myself.

Caroline B. Cooney is the author of many books for young people, including *If the Witness Lied; Diamonds in the Shadow; A Friend at Midnight; Hit the Road; Code Orange; The Girl Who Invented Romance; Family Reunion; Goddess of Yesterday* (an ALA-ALSC Notable Children's Book); *The Ransom of Mercy Carter; Tune In Anytime; Burning Up; The Face on the Milk Carton* (an IRA-CBC Children's Choice Book) and its companions, *Whatever Happened to Janie?* and *The Voice on the Radio* (each of them an ALA-YALSA Best Book for Young Adults), as well as *What Janie Found; What Child Is This?* (an ALA-YALSA Best Book for Young Adults); *Driver's Ed* (an ALA-YALSA Best Book for Young Adults and a *Booklist* Editors' Choice); *Among Friends; Twenty Pageants Later;* and the Time Travel Quartet: *Both Sides of Time, Out of Time, Prisoner of Time,* and *For All Time,* which are also available as *The Time Travelers,* Volumes I and II.

Caroline B. Cooney lives in South Carolina and New York.